ROLLER SKATES
Ruth Sawyer

A year on roller skates! That was Lucinda's year in New York City, when her family left her with dear Miss Peters, who understood that a girl of ten wanted to roller-skate to school, and who wasn't always worrying about a little lady's social dignity. At that time in the 1890s Lucinda could explore the special places in New York, and make friends with all the different neighborhood characters, from the junkman, old Rags-an'-Bottles, to Patrolman M'Gonegal and the hansom cab driver, Mr. Gilligan. This is a delightful story of old New York, about a tomboy who could not help being a lady at the same time, who was both quick-tempered and sympathetic, both stubborn and clever.

ROLLER SKATES

WRITTEN BY RUTH SAWYER AND
ILLUSTRATED BY VALENTI ANGELO

PUFFIN BOOKS

CONTENTS

AN INTRODUCTION TO LUCINDA   3

I   UP DRIVES MR. GILLIGAN   7

II   FRIEND AT LARGE   26

III   AN EXCITING MEETING
WITH MR. WILLIAM SHAKESPEARE   47

IV   MOSTLY RUBBISH   67

V   THANKSGIVING   85

VI   BORN IS THE KING OF ISRAEL   103

VII   TWELFTH NIGHT   120

VIII   ROLLER SKATES   138

IX   A GULL FLIES SEAWARD   155

X   AWAY GOES LUCINDA   172

ROLLER
SKATES

AN INTRODUCTION TO LUCINDA

SPRING has come; windows are open. Green fire burns fiercely along the branches of every tree and shrub. A month ago the wild geese started flying north; over the lake, against a morning sky, the black-dotted wedge of their flying made lovely patterns. Birds have all picked their house sites among hedgerows and tree-tops. They are hard at work discovering their own building material. Our neighbor's bees are singing their spring foraging song. The little brown bee does hum—ho-hum.

Through the open window comes the sound of roller

skates. Along the macadam road, where by law or caution they should not be, children dart back and forth like low-skimming swallows. Clump—chug—chirr—clump! Arms saw the air. The plaids and checks, the skirts and sweaters, make patterns. A red-head unties a skipping rope from around her waist and thrusts the wooden handles into two hands outstretched to receive them. In a moment she is going to show what can be done on roller skates with a skipping rope.

A solitary figure escapes the huddle. She chugs over to the curb and mounts it to the sidewalk. She stands there and shows what a strange little figure she is, different from the rest. She wears a pongee pinafore, buttoned down the back and with long sleeves. She wears a navy-blue sailor hat with ribbons down the back, held under the chin with an elastic band. She wears ribbed black stockings and high black laced shoes with stubby toes, badly barked.

I know her in an instant; although I had forgotten all about her for years, had forgotten she ever existed. It gives me a shock to see her, looking so exactly as she should look, so everlastingly full of life and still on roller skates. I put my head out of the window and call:

"Lucinda!"

She comes as if she had been expecting that call. She chugs up the lawn to my window and tilts up to me a face wearing an impish grin. Her mother and mine used to catch the reflection of it so often in the mirror when Lucinda was brushing her short-cropped hair with a bang.

"What brought you back?" I ask.

Lucinda waves a hand towards the huddle of skaters. "Those—thousands and thousands of them, coming out fresh

every spring like the crocuses. Roller skates—all going somewhere. Don't you remember that year?"

How had I forgotten it!

I was ashamed and covered it, reminding her, "But it
wasn't spring then."

"No, it was September. But it was spring that I skated
away and never really came back." Her face had lost its grin;
it was very eager now. "Don't you remember?"

We were very quiet—I, leaning over the window-sill, Lucinda, craning her neck up at me. I could see disappointment,
and something deeper spread over her face. "You've forgotten. How could you! It was the loveliest—the very loveliest
year of all."

"I'm remembering." I could, in fact, suddenly see her
skating down Fifth Avenue, coasting into that part of Bryant
Park that the New York Public Library was later to snatch
away. "What was that policeman's name, Lucinda?"

"Patrolman M'Gonegal!" She was indignant. "I suppose
you've forgotten Tony and the Coppinos. You've even forgotten Mr. Gilligan and his hansom cab."

I had; and Lucinda read it from my face. "Didn't you keep
the diary?"

I had. Where was it? "Wait a moment," I called. I went
rummaging in closets and drawers and desks; and came upon
it—a small, red leather book with "My Diary" written slantwise across the cover. I showed it to Lucinda through the
window.

"Well, you haven't lost it, at any rate." She said it tartly.
"That ought to help you remember a lot. Open it!"

My fingers turned pages. I read scatterings here and there.

Names jumped out at me: Miss Lucy, honey—Pygmalion—
Aleda—the Princess Zayda—Trinket. Memories came back
like homing birds. "What did ever happen to Mr. Night
Owl?" I asked.

Lucinda gave a satisfied smile. "I thought I ought to come
back and start your memory off on roller skates, too." The
impish grin was back. "Turn to the first page, begin at the
beginning."

So I turned to the first page and read the date: "September
11th, 189—"

CHAPTER I

UP DRIVES MR. GILLIGAN

IT was Patrick Gilligan in his hansom cab who took Lucinda around from the old Gedney House to the Misses Peters' apartment, two flights up. Chance was good to them both, as Mr. Gilligan was in the habit of pointing out to Lucinda afterwards. It would have been a great pity entirely if they had never met, "you bein' ten past an' me fifty past— the right ages, just, to get well acquainted."

Lucinda's father had intended to take her around on the hoof, as Lucinda put it, with the hotel porter taking her baggage over later. But just as they were leaving, Aunt Emily interfered. Aunt Emily had spent a lifetime interfering— days—weeks—years. There was nothing she could do better, or that she enjoyed more. To thrust her finger into somebody's pie and wreck it—that was Aunt Emily for you. Lucinda's grandmother, having died when her mother was a very little girl, had left Aunt Emily the oldest of the family; and to her had descended that divine right of putting her finger into family pies.

Lucinda had said good-bye without tears to her mother; she did not believe in weeping over sensible events. As she and her father were making for the door of their hotel sitting-room, Lucinda's mother flung after them the advice she thought was most important: "Don't forget Sundays—church or Sunday School—I don't care which you choose. And don't forget Aunt Emily's every Saturday for sewing and supper. Be mama's good little girl and try not to have tantrums. Write often in your diary. Oh, yes, and don't forget to put on your underdrawers by the last of October."

They opened the door and there stood a messenger boy, about to knock. He delivered a letter to Lucinda's mother in Aunt Emily's handwriting. And when Lucinda's father saw it he said to the boy: "You'd better wait for an answer"; and to Lucinda: "We'd better go back and sit down. Something is bound to happen."

So back they went, and with trembling fingers Lucinda's mother opened the letter and read it aloud:

"*My dear Bessie:*

If you and Dr. Hitchcock think your health depends on your going off suddenly like this, without consulting me and abandoning your only daughter, I beg of you to abandon her to relatives. Miss Peters is an excellent woman, no doubt, and admirable as a teacher; but she is hardly the person to have the guidance of a child like Lucinda for approximately a year. I am very fond of Lucinda; but you know as well as I do that she is headstrong, and far too independent and out-spoken. I believe in calling a spade a spade."

At this point Lucinda's mother looked up with a stricken face. "I never imagined that Sister Emily would take it this way."

"She was bound to, but I thought we should get away ahead of her. Read on, my dear." And Lucinda's father put a sustaining arm about Lucinda's mother while she read on:

"Miss Peters has no social position. She knows no more about the social training and behavior demanded in a daughter of a family in our position than she does about breeding Belgian hares."

This time Lucinda's father brought the reading to a full stop. He chuckled, "I should say Emily was getting vulgar."

Lucinda's mother said, "Frank—please!" And went on with the letter:

"Lucinda can share the room with Frances and Virginia. It will not be overly convenient to have a fifth child in the house; nevertheless, I insist that you send her to us. I shall find adequate compensation in whatever inconvenience there may be in the thought of having Lucinda under my constant eye, under the careful supervision of mam'selle, and in the daily companionship of my own docile and ladylike daughters. Can I say more?"

She did, for four more pages. Before the letter was finished

Lucinda's mother was reduced to weeping, her father to anger, and Lucinda herself to open mutiny.

"How can I go and leave Lucinda behind after that letter!" moaned her mother.

"You'll have to forget it. It so happens that you have got to be taken away; that our passage has been bought; the ship sails in an hour; and for once Emily is not going to interfere with our plans." Her father pounded his fist on the table.

"But Lucinda? She is headstrong—we know that. I can't go against Sister Emily's wishes. I shall have to send her. Oh, Frank, what shall we do?"

It was at this point that Lucinda mutinied. She bounced up and down like a rebellious rubber ball. "I tell you I won't go to Aunt Emily's! I'll run away if you send me there. She'll own me—legs, arms, and French verbs. Not an inch of me will belong to myself. I'd rather be dead than live with Aunt Emily and her four docile, ladylike daughters." Lucinda minced the last words in shameful, impertinent mimicry.

For once she went unreprimanded. The emergency was too great, time too scarce. Lucinda's father took her by the hand, speaking to her mother: "Write a note and say our arrangements are final. I'll have to send Lucinda off by herself in a cab. If we make the boat now it will be by the grace of God and nothing else."

The messenger boy helped. Lucinda's baggage was piled into the hotel elevator; the porter was shouted for; Timmy Hicks, the Buttons, who was a special friend of Lucinda's, came on the run. Even the manager appeared. Lucinda's exit from the Gedney House took on something of a Roman conqueror's triumphal procession. There was the messenger

boy with a dangling strapful of books and more books braced against a shoulder. The porter with a small brass-bound trunk on his back. It had been Lucinda's mother's wedding trunk, and Lucinda had begged it for her own. Brass nail-heads spangled the top as stars the firmament. Her father followed carrying a traveling desk, covered with fine, green morocco; this was a parting gift to Lucinda from both parents. He carried as well, and with difficulty, a contraption covered over with a length of a discarded plush parlor curtain of a rich old-gold color, and in addition he managed a pasteboard box that clicked and rattled as he walked. Next came

Timmy Hicks, lugging the Gladstone bag not half an inch from the floor.

Lucinda, like Abou ben Adhem, led all the rest. She carried a pair of new roller skates over one shoulder and clutched in her other hand a guitar.

The hotel manager, Mr. Spindler, kind, solicitous, was saying to Lucinda's father: "Let me help you with some of those bundles, Mr. Wyman. I promise we'll keep an eye on Lucinda, Mrs. Spindler and I, even if she isn't living in the house. Don't worry. You've no idea how much store my wife sets by the child. She'll always be welcome."

Timmy Hicks was hurrying to catch up with Lucinda before old Charlie, the doorman, should let her out. He made a whispered shouting with his voice. "Say, Lucinda, you'll come back sometimes, won't you? Say you will—honest Injun!"

"Honest Injun."

Fat little Mrs. Caldwell with her tiny dog, Pygmalion, came out of the dining-room in time to see the procession. She stopped to kiss Lucinda good-bye. "Pygmalion and I will miss you. Promise to come back and see us often."

"I promise."

Old Charlie opened the door. Lucinda's father shouted, "Get us a cab, Charlie!" And at that very moment Mr. Gilligan in his hansom cab was driving leisurely by, looking for a fare.

He drove up to the curb; and everybody had a hand in performing the miracle. While the cab teetered on its two wheels, inside went Lucinda, the wedding trunk, the Gladstone bag, the covered contraption, the pasteboard box, books, skates, guitar.

Lucinda's father was on the step, kissing Lucinda good-bye, patting her cheeks, saying: "Don't miss us. Have a rousing time. You'll never be free like this again."

And old Charlie was saying: "Don't you worry none, Mr. Wyman, that chile 'll land on her two feet no matter where she drops from or to. You could sling her over Madison Square and she'd come down feet first."

And Mr. Gilligan was saying, "Giddap," and cracking his whip. No one had thought to tell him where Lucinda was going. So he hailed her from aloft: "Where to, Miss?"

"To Rome," laughed Lucinda, thinking of the triumphal procession. She looked overhead to make sure where the voice was coming from and saw the round face of a wrinkled and rosy angel, surmounted by a shiny high hat, peering down at her. Solemnly she gave Miss Peters' street and number and added: "Two flights up."

She heard the square opening above being slammed shut; and stood it for one block of slow jogging. Then she jabbed at it with the handle of her guitar. After all, such an occasion called for company and conversation.

The window opened, the face appeared. "I'm takin' ye the right way, Miss."

"I know you are; but keep it open. I want to talk," and Lucinda beamed back at the wrinkled angel. Mr. Gilligan had to turn a corner just then, but as soon as they were safely around Lucinda shouted for attention: "I've joined the orphanage. The last five minutes have made me an orphan."

"Dear me," said Mr. Gilligan, "as sad as that!"

"It isn't sad at all. I think it's going to be awfully pleasant. That is—if I can manage to escape Aunt Emily. She may get me yet—as the goblins got Little Orphant Annie."

"Dear me," said Mr. Gilligan for the second time, feeling confused.

Sliding down on her spine, the better to tilt her head up to meet the voice of Mr. Gilligan, Lucinda shouted in a slowly rising crescendo: "I'm not a permanent orphan. My father and mother have gone abroad—at least they are about to go abroad. You know—Latin grammar—'The farmer is about to cultivate the field.' My father is an importer. My mother has a kind of illness; it makes her live in Italy, but she doesn't have to stay in bed. Ever been there?"

"Meaning bed?" carefully inquired the voice.

Lucinda was on the point of answering indignantly, but she looked first and caught the grin on the face peering down at her. It made her grin back. "What's your name?"

"Patrick Gilligan."

"Irish." Lucinda spoke the word with relish. "I had an Irish nurse till I was eight—Johanna. Now she's second girl. I'd rather have an Irish nurse than a French governess any day. Johanna came from County Antrim. Ever been there?"

He never had. County Wicklow was his; and County Kerry was Mrs. Gilligan's.

"Have you fairy raths in your counties? And do you make griddle bread there, with currants in it?"

"Fairies and currant bread every night—if you like," agreed Mr. Gilligan.

Lucinda's heart leaped upward to meet the heart of Mr.

Gilligan somewhere outside the hansom cab. If Mr. Gilligan had a Mrs. Gilligan, perhaps some night they might invite her to their house to have griddle bread with currants in it—and a cup of tea. Suddenly she felt as if she wanted that to happen more than anything else in the world. Suddenly she felt very alone—a single pea in a pod that had only a short time ago held two parents, four brothers, a French governess, Jo, the cook, Johanna, the one-time nurse, and Connelly, the odd-man. And the pod had shrunk from a full-sized house to a hansom cab—moving in space. She clutched her guitar and looked with suspense about her to make sure that nothing of what she had brought with her to tie her safely to the past had been jolted out. Satisfied, her mind traveled back to the griddle bread and she shouted eagerly: "You cut it pie-ways and eat it hot off the griddle."

"With plenty of butter." Above Mr. Gilligan smacked his lips.

They had reached the given street and number. Mr. Gilligan got down with difficulty. He was small and stoutish and fitted snug in the cab-top. He snapped a leather strap on to the bridle of his horse; and flung it, with a weight at the other end, to the ground. "There, she'll stand, easy as a cricket. Now out you come—upsy-downsy," and he jumped Lucinda over her baggage to the pavement.

It took two trips to the second floor before everything was up. Miss Peters and Miss Nettie, a younger sister, were there to receive them. Everything was stowed away in the front room which was a parlor and had lots of furniture and what-nots. This room, Lucinda was given to understand, was to be mostly hers.

"Oh, but I couldn't think of taking it," said Lucinda in the best family manner; and then she introduced Mr. Gilligan to the two ladies.

Miss Peters said: "I'm sure it's very kind of you, Mr. Gilligan, to take all this trouble."

"None at all, ma'am." He was putting the covered contraption into a corner and removing his high hat for the first time—that having been impossible before. He stood there looking very pink and wrinkled and full of pleasure. "If I thought I was not makin' too bold, ma'am, I'd like to be askin' the young lady to tea some night, currant bread having been mentioned between us, as you might say." At this he ceased addressing Miss Peters and doubled up half-shut, to grin again into Lucinda's face, "Cut pie-ways with plenty of butter."

Lucinda rose on the stubby ends of her shoes in complete ecstasy. "Oh, please, Miss Peters! You see Mr. Gilligan is a friend of mine and I'm sure mama would want me to go and have tea with him and Mrs. Gilligan. Irish both of them— County Wicklow and County Kerry." Lucinda could not have said it with more manner if she had been saying: "Fifth Avenue and Tuxedo."

The eyes of Miss Peters questioned the eyes of Miss Nettie; but whatever doubts she may have had she kept to herself. She was, as Lucinda was to prove her throughout that heavenly year, a person of great understanding, no nonsense, and no interference. She spoke as to an equal:

"I am sure Lucinda would enjoy it very much. Will you escort her, Mr. Gilligan?"

"Naught less," he agreed. Then he bowed and the ladies

bowed and Lucinda bowed, only to straighten up quickly that she might hang over the banisters and see the last of Mr. Gilligan vanish through the door below.

Blissfully unhampered, Lucinda was left for the rest of the afternoon to explore her new home and settle her belongings. She adored packing and unpacking and did it neatly. She was not so successful at everyday tidiness.

Like a young rock-codling she darted in and out of recesses, cupboards, closets, and bureau drawers. The home of the Misses Peters, which she learned so soon to call "ours," consisted of the whole second floor—parlor, bedroom, workroom, and bathroom. The latter was not wholly theirs. The work-room was small, and excited Lucinda's admiration and interest. It followed Johanna's description of a wee Irish cabin: you could stand in the middle and without stirring foot put the kettle on the fire, the dishes on the dresser, the crock under the table, and lift the latch on the door.

Miss Nettie went out by the day to sew; and sometimes she brought sewing home with her to finish. The work-room held a sewing machine and ironing board, a shelf on which stood a double gas-plate for cooking, a cupboard for dishes, a closet for linen, and a curtained corner for broom and dustpan and carpet-sweeper. A small cutting table with legs that folded up stood against the wall; and there was a row of plants on the window ledge. "Snug, I call it," said Lucinda. "Can I call it my work-room, too?"

It seemed that she could. She set to work to put her things in their places; and the amazing little room stretched itself to hold them all. The covered contraption was a toy theater—packed to its doors with actors and scenery, temporarily out of work. The pasteboard box held Lucinda's large-sized dolls' dishes—white English china with orange bands around the edges. They were among her most treasured possessions, along with the knives, forks, and spoons, and the basket that held them. Dishes were moved in the cupboard to make room for hers on the lowest shelf, easily reached. There were as well two teacloths and napkins for four to match. Miss Nettie opened the cutting table to see if the cloths would fit. They did—exactly.

Lucinda was to have her supper on that cutting table every night—at six sharp. She could choose what teacloth and what dishes she would like, anything from the cupboard but the old English Spode from the top shelf. She could mostly choose what she would like for supper, too. The Misses Peters took their dinner downstairs in the boarding house— which was two houses.

"I hope you won't mind having your supper alone?" asked Miss Nettie, timidly. She was naturally timid as compared to Miss Peters, robust and secure. She knew very little about children; Miss Peters knew a great deal, especially about girls, having taught them all her life. Children interested Miss Peters, especially when she found one that had not been run into a mold or cut out of a given piece of cloth and made up like a flannel rabbit. That was why she had consented to Lucinda. Miss Nettie wanted for once to be near enough to some child to know her well enough to love. In her secret heart she hoped Lucinda would not mind being that child. But she was prepared to begin timidly with her. She raised her voice a little and asked her question again: "I hope you won't mind having supper alone."

"I'm used to it. Of course my mam'selle had it with me in the nursery. But she—" Lucinda abandoned her with a generous sweep of an arm. She hoped she was through forever with French governesses.

The pinnacle of that first day of orphanage for Lucinda was discovering her bed. There was a run-way between the parlor and the bedroom, occupied by the Misses Peters; and in it there were two wardrobes, two cupboards with shelves and drawers; and in between a washstand with running water. Here Lucinda had put away all her clothes. In the parlor a table had been set aside to hold her desk; a shelf had been cleared for her books. "But where," asked Lucinda, "do I sleep? It's very mysterious." The sofa had been tested by eye; but it had been discarded as not exactly a bed for the winter.

Miss Nettie, chirruping now with delight, drew back some plush curtains from what was intended to look like a curtained bookcase. She pressed something and down came a bed—an ample bed with legs to stand on, mattress, sheets, blankets, pillows, everything complete.

"I never saw one like it. What do you call it?" Lucinda was enthralled.

"It's a folding bed."

"Will it fold up with me in it?"

"Heaven forbid!"

"I wish Heaven wouldn't. It would be fun." Lucinda was disappointed. Having a lively imagination she could picture herself, with head placed to the front, rising as by magic until nothing could be seen but her head protruding from the top. By this performance she could appear as one of Bluebeard's beheaded wives. But disappointment did not last. "I think I shall go to bed early, right after supper. I'm awfully excited. I want to see what it feels like to sleep in a folding bed."

After supper, however, Lucinda dawdled. She wanted to feel to the utmost the delicious strangeness and difference of everything. There were her books, too, to put on their shelf; and there was the new diary that her mother had bought her and that she had promised to write in often. The books she handled and put in their places with loving care. They filled a large portion of her inner world—a sanctuary built securely to keep out Aunt Emilys and French governesses. She smoothed her copy of *Tanglewood Tales*, with a gold Pegasus riding over a crimson cover; she patted *Water Babies*, without pictures and a feckless binding that matched *The King of The Golden River* and *Plutarch's Lives*. There was *Hans Andersen*, with a frontispiece of Little Ida and her flowers. Every story Andersen had written was in the book; and Lucinda had read them all since her tenth birthday. Next came *Alice's Adventures in Wonderland*. Secretly Lucinda laid her own claim to the adventures, so many times had she followed the White Rabbit down the hole, swum the pool of Alice's tears, read the labels and drunk from the two bottles, been invited by the Queen of Hearts to play croquet, with a flamingo for a mallet. Beside Alice, on the shelf, went *The Peterkin Papers*; and next to that her beloved *Uncle Remus*, *Hans Brinker*, *Jan of the Windmill*, *Robin Hood*, and *Swiss Family Robinson*.

Three books were left—the three that came most often to Lucinda's book-itching fingers. A worn, calf-bound dictionary. She had begged it from her oldest brother when he had turned in his college books and started for Idaho and gold-mining. Words—just words, waiting to be hung into sentences—fascinated Lucinda. She had made any number of games out of that dictionary: the game of discovering new words, the game of jumbling them into rhymes the way Curdy did to frighten the goblins, the game of twenty questions that she played with a brand-new word to see if the elders in her household knew what it meant. She divided the books upstanding on the shelves and laid the dictionary flat between them. Upon it she put *Our Boys in India*—as full of pictures as a rice pudding should be full of raisins—and wandering through the pages of it her mysterious Dhondaram. The last book she opened at random, as from long habit. It didn't matter where her fingers found a place in the story of Diamond it was sure to catch her up and carry her off with him to the back of the North Wind. Now she opened and read aloud the singing words:

" '*Please North Wind,*' *he said,* '*what is that noise?*' *From high over his head came the voice of North Wind answering him gently,* '*The noise of my besom. I am the old woman who sweeps the cobwebs from the sky; only I'm busy with the floor now.*'

" '*What makes the houses look as if they were running away?*'

" '*I am sweeping so fast over them.*' "

Lucinda read on, loving the feeling of words on her tongue, and the dancing lilt of the sentences. So, coming up from their dinner, did the Misses Peters find her, sitting cross-legged on the floor, bent nearly double like a Parker House roll. She raised a contented face to theirs, "I expect I'm going to love living with you, Miss Peters, Miss Nettie. It's all so handy, and all the things I love best are right around me, and I have a folding bed to sleep in, think of that! I've joined a lucky orphanage."

Miss Peters offered to hear her say her prayers every night, but Lucinda gently but firmly preferred to say them to herself. Miss Nettie reminded her that if she felt lonely she could creep into bed with her. Lucinda thanked her and refused. "I shall always sleep alone until I'm married; then I suppose I shall have to sleep with my husband. Everybody does that, I know."

After that she undressed; putting her pongee pinafore and her dress over the back of the chair, her underwaist, petticoat, drawers, and vest on the seat, her stockings, criss-cross, and turned inside out to air, over the arms; and on the floor, her shoes, heel to heel, with stubby toes pointing outwards in the exact position recommended by Dodworth in dancing school. This was going-to-bed ritual, trained into Lucinda through many years of effort by Johanna.

Around Lucinda's neck was still a narrow ribbon that she had worn all day. At the end of it hung a tiny brass key. It was the key to her desk—her precious new desk. She intended to keep it locked always; and to keep inside her secret things. No one should ever know what the desk might gather unto itself down the years to come. No one—ever, should ever know! Not until she was married, anyway. Then, probably, she would have to take the key—like this, open the desk, and say to her husband: "Behold the secrets of my life!"

The idea so thrilled Lucinda that it was a long while before she could get down to the business of writing in the diary. It was new, like the desk. It was bound in red leather and had "My Diary" written across the cover, slantwise. Inside, the pages were ruled. Lucinda felt the deep importance of the moment—to be writing her name inside: "Lucinda Wyman," and on the opposite page, at the top, "September 11th, 189—"

When she had finished she locked it safely away again. She took off wrapper and slippers, climbed the straight-backed chair to reach the gas jet, and turned it off. Pale light from the street-lamps below came through the two windows and revealed the folding bed, unfolded, waiting for her. She caught at the moment; spreading her arms like stubby wings, she sprang from the chair and aimed headlong for the bed.

The impact on landing raised such a racket that the Misses Peters came on the run. Every ornament on the what-nots was chattering; the pictures on the walls beat a gentle tattoo. "Whatever has happened? Lucinda are you hurt?" First Miss Peters' affirmative voice, then Miss Nettie's timid one.

Lucinda giggled. "I've just been flying. I take to it at odd moments—when I'm up on something high. You mustn't let it disturb you. I'll probably do a lot of flying this winter—I always seem just about to be getting the hang of it. Good night, Miss Peters. Good night, Miss Nettie. Did you ever try flying when you were around ten?"

New York City, Sept. 11th, 189—
Well it's all over and done. A good thing too. When you
become an orphan you want to become one quick, without
tears. If it hadn't been for Aunt Emily there wouldn't have
been any. Poor mama—papa and I escaped.
I think Aunt Emily's bound to stir up Heaven when she
gets there. Maybe she won't ever get there. That will be a joke
on Aunt Emily.
Mr. Gilligan is the best Handsome Cab Driver in New York
City. He's what you would call made for it. He belongs inside his cab just as a mermaid belongs inside her tail. He gives
you such a surprise when he climbs out and you discover he
has legs. I hope he won't forget about tea and griddle bread.
It would be a great disappointment if he did. It's going to be
comfortable here. I don't think I shall have many tantrums.
I won't have mam'selle shouting at me Vite-Vite every minute. I like Miss Peters. Her house manner is better than her
school manner. But I think I'm going to like Miss Nettie
most. She's so disturbed for fear I will miss mama and papa
and get homesick and mind things. I told her I didn't mind
anything in the world but being fussed over, Aunt Emily,
mad dogs and tripe. I think it's wicked to make children
eat tripe.
Being an orphan makes you feel elegant—like being Dick
Whittington. Only I have no cat; and no bells rang for me
when I rode up in Mr. Gilligan's Handsome Cab.
I don't think my flying is improving any—I kerplunk as bad

as ever, but I'm going to keep right on trying. With a folding bed of my own and no mam'selle around to snoop I can practice a lot.

Well the morning and the evening was the first day— as it says in the Bible; and I feel just like the King of the Castle without any dirty rascal to cope with. Cope is my latest word.

CHAPTER II

FRIEND AT LARGE

EVERY morning —Monday to Friday—Lucinda skated to school. School was private and belonged to Anna
C. Brackett, a person both terrible and wonderful and always
to be reckoned with. Lucinda had much the same feeling
about Miss Brackett as she had about God. She was everywhere; she knew everything; and she couldn't be fooled.

Miss Peters taught in the school, and every morning that was fair or tolerable she and Lucinda started out together. They arrived together, but the distance between they took each at her own pace. At the end of the first block on the cross-street, Lucinda would take the curb at a jump, wave a farewell hand, shout: "See you there, Miss Peters," and away she would go. Chug—clump—chirr—clump! That was the last Miss Peters would hear of her. The last she would see was a swaying figure in a pongee pinafore, buttoned up the back, a navy-blue sailor, sailing off her head but anchored to her by a stout elastic band under her chin. Arms would be waving like the churning paddles of a side-wheeler.

But the first thing Patrolman M'Gonegal would see was a half-squatting figure, hands on knees, skates close together, coasting through the entrance to Bryant Park; taking the curves westward without a stumble and coming to a final stop with a very unladylike: "Whoop!" It was at the corner of Fortieth Street that Lucinda would pick up Miss Peters again, and they would take the final block in company; Lucinda moderating, Miss Peters accelerating, and both making the most of equality. The equality vanished, once inside the door on Thirty-Ninth Street.

Patrolman M'Gonegal's beat was Bryant Park, and that stretch of Fifth Avenue that bound it. He had marked Lucinda long before, and without interest, as a child of society, going down the avenue, pulling at the hand of a rigid Frenchwoman like a puppy on a leash. But the leash had been slipped; the puppy was free, and he watched for her every morning with a sense of deep satisfaction. Young things shouldn't be tied up. Didn't he know it—he had three of his own. A city like New York wasn't too big to turn them loose in—barring a few corners of it. He had been waiting for a week to pick Lucinda's acquaintance when she gave him the chance by catching her skate on the curb and plunging head-long into the traffic of the street.

She let out a yelp like a frightened puppy and Patrolman M'Gonegal held up two delivery carts, pulled her to her feet, set her down upon the opposite curb, and asked: "Hurt?"

"Not a mite. The breath's just blown out of me." She looked down at the pongee pinafore. "That's ruined. Glory be to God, I can go one day without it."

The policeman was brushing her off and eyeing her with pleasure: "Glory be to God, yourself, and are you Irish?"

"Almost," said Lucinda. "I had an Irish wet nurse when I was a baby; and until I was eight I had a dry nurse, Johanna —straight from County Antrim."

"I'm Irish myself. Patrolman M'Gonegal—at your service."

"Thank you. I always did want to know your name."

He pulled a small brown paper bag out of his pocket and offered Lucinda a lime drop. "Green's my color," he laughed, "and I've a sweet tooth. It helps pass the time."

Miss Peters came upon them one morning in serious con-versation over English sparrows. Lucinda introduced them. Miss Peters acknowledged the introduction graciously but once out of earshot she remonstrated: "Lucinda, you simply can't make friends with all the policemen and all the cab drivers in New York."

"Only one of each," she reminded Miss Peters.

"Are you going to make the acquaintance of everyone in the park? They're mostly tramps, you know."

"There is one awfully nice one—old and very much a gentleman. I've already made his acquaintance. I gave him a nickel the other day for a cup of coffee. You have no idea how pleased he was."

Miss Peters was about to be very angry. Her face had gotten red and she stopped Lucinda in the middle of the block and looked at her severely. Lucinda looked back with eyes that did not waver—having nothing about which to waver. Miss Peters groaned helplessly. "It had better be cab drivers and policemen. Lucinda, you simply can't go about making friends with everybody. Think of what your Aunt Emily would say if she knew."

"That's just it. I've had too much of Aunt Emily all my life. You have no idea how much I enjoy these other friends I'm making."

But Miss Peters was firm. She explained that she did not question the manners of the tramp who had been treated to a cup of coffee; others might not turn out so pleasant, however. Lucinda must promise to leave the loafers in Bryant Park, or anywhere else, strictly alone. Lucinda promised; both knew the promise would be kept, no matter how regretfully.

Lucinda was never to know until she was grown how many conferences the Misses Peters held after she had gone to bed. "We must be firm with her," they said it often to each other —firmly. They recalled often what her parents had said: "You must keep Lucinda in hand or she will run the city," this from her father; "You must punish her often," this from her mother.

"Not punish her," Miss Nettie always urged timidly. "She

is such a reasonable child." But in spite of their best intentions, they could not allow themselves to dam up that clear, vigorous flood of life in Lucinda that had impelled her to buckle on roller skates and sweep the city like a small, square-toed, square-cut, Winged Victory on wheels.

Like the bottom dropping out of a cheese-box, the dos and don'ts dropped out of the daily vocabulary that had heretofore confronted Lucinda. There were certain things discussed by Miss Peters, and agreed upon mutually, as necessary for the peace of mind and welfare of the three of them. So on the table beside Lucinda's desk was placed a pad and pencil. After she had returned from school and had had her dinner, Lucinda was to write down what she proposed to do for the afternoon. So could Miss Peters know of her whereabouts, and incidentally, judge how Lucinda's afternoons were being spent, and with whom. She was always to be home by five-thirty.

In their turn, Miss Peters and Miss Nettie were to write of their plans, so that Lucinda could know. "It's an elegant arrangement," said Lucinda. "Everybody as free as air, and yet all of us polite about it. How ever did you think it up, Miss Peters?"

Their house and the house next door was run by a Miss Lucy Wimple, known to the inmates and boarders as "Miss Lucy, honey," because that was what her faithful black Susan called her. Black Susan was cook; and she had come up from Virginia with Miss Lucy from the old home to make a living for both of them. It was at Miss Lucy's table that Lucinda had her midday dinners; without the Misses Peters who never came back until late afternoon. Lucinda found the boarders exciting, messed up together, like a game of jack-straws. It was exciting to pick them out one by one and put them into two piles: the ones she liked, the ones she didn't.

Next to her, at the table, sat a young man who never got up until noon; and usually came down with sleepy eyes and sandy hair that stood upright over his head.

"Well, who are you, new one?" he asked, blinking at Lucinda, her first noon down.

Lucinda gave him a lengthy account and in turn asked about him. She believed that friendships, to begin well, had to stand on mutual information and plenty of it.

"Well, my name's Hugh Marshall, newspaper reporter. I work nights and so I'm a night owl." To prove it, he separated two stalks from his shock of hair, and twisted them until they stood upright and pointed at the corners of his head. Lucinda adored him on the spot and called him Mr. Night Owl.

Across the table from her sat a wisp of a woman—a little old Irish fairy woman she might have been, with her white hair, her wizened face and her young eyes. Everybody called her "Lady Ross" as if it must be true. Mr. Night Owl told a scrap of her history to Lucinda in the hallway, afterwards. Lady Ross had never gone back to Ireland after her husband had died. He had been wealthy, had owned racing horses, and had brought them over to this country to Saratoga for the big summer seasons. In time, Lady Ross invited Lucinda to come into the house next door, where she had her rooms, and there she would tell stories as wonderful as any Johanna knew. She was like a living picture-book, for she made the pictures appear with the telling of each story until Lucinda could see what manner of lad Oisin was, and Fionn Mac-

Cumal—and all the old Irish heroes. She gave Lucinda a new
word for fairy—*shee*—that sounded so fairyish on her tongue.
She told of the white fairy, the banshee, that calls the death
of a strong man in Ireland. She taught Lucinda the banshee's
call; a wailing cry like the call of a loon at night, only with
more wildness to it. She spoke with a soft Galway brogue that
Lucinda could imitate before she had been near her a week.
And Lady Ross had never lost the way of young laughter.

The very first time that Lucinda skated up with Mr. Gilligan, on Broadway and without a fare, Lucinda hailed him
and tried on him that Galway brogue. It set Mr. Gilligan off
into spasms which almost shook him out of the cab-top.
"You're as Irish as if ye were born there," he roared. Often of
a fine afternoon did they pick up each other in this fashion
and talk of matters that might have covered a map. When
Mr. Gilligan had a fare he passed Lucinda with nothing more
than a grin and the flick of his whip. But either way—stopping or passing—the very sight of him warmed the cockles of
her heart, and Lucinda would say to herself in the manner of
a grand lady: "There goes my friend, Mr. Gilligan, best hansom cab driver in New York City."

Fall weather was the best weather for making friends. You
met everybody coming or going; met them alive and eager
and made friendly by the gently keen September air. She
made friends with three lodgers from the third floor who
never came to Miss Lucy's table. She had passed them several
times on the stoop, in the street, on the stairs, before she
made their acquaintance. One was a tall, thready man with
eyes that burned as round and black as Lucinda's own, with
hollow cheeks that made his face gaunt and mysterious. One

was a not-so-tall woman; young, with a worried face and pretty lips that seemed to be always holding something back. Between them, a hand to each, came the third one; not bigger than a pint-pot, Lucinda thought. Her little face was very solemn, and under the dark-blue bonnet she wore hung long curls, the color of true gold.

They were coming downstairs one day; Lucinda was going up, her skates over her shoulder, jangling noisily. Impulsively Lucinda dropped the skates, knelt on the stairs and blocked the way of the three. Her face wore its impish grin. She held out both hands, cupped as if to catch something. "I want some gold—some truly gold," she said. And then, "So pretty. What's your name?"

"Trinket," said the little girl.

"Caroline Browdowski," said the woman, "but she is our very own trinket. It's a pet name."

"Oh! I never had a pet name. I'm called Lucinda, and sometimes severely—Lucinda Wyman! And I never had curls, either."

Lucinda's sailor hat was hanging around her neck by its elastic as usual. The man put his hand on her close-cropped, black hair. "It suits you better not to have curls, I think. Feel it, my dear," he said to the woman, "it is as fine and sleek as a raven's breast."

The words sang themselves straight into Lucinda's heart. No one had ever said nice things about her hair before, or about anything else that made up Lucinda, for that matter. Aunt Emily referred to her often and openly as "homely as two toads." It had never seemed to be important what people thought of her, especially what Aunt Emily thought until one day last summer. Lucinda was going to a party—along with her four cousins—"the docile, ladylike daughters" of Aunt Emily—Frances, Virginia, Sybil, and Agatha. They all looked very elegant, with ribbon sashes and hair ribbons. Aunt Emily had looked at Lucinda and the absence of all ribbons, and had said it again.

Something had gone off inside of Lucinda like fireworks and she had stamped her foot and shouted, "Glory be to God, Aunt Emily, if you must say it keep it down to one toad! I'm sick to death of two!"

For that tantrum mama had kept her home from the party and sent her early to bed.

Now Lucinda was looking up at the hollow-cheeked compelling face leaning over her, and she knew for the first time how much she wanted those she liked to like her—to discover something nice about her, such as hair, "fine and sleek as a raven's breast." The words repeated themselves inside to Lucinda. Suddenly she felt so grateful. She wanted these three, too, for friends; especially the one pint-pot size. "I live under you," she said. "We're what you'd call neighbors. Could I borrow Trinket sometimes?"

The man and woman looked at each other as if something strange had happened to them. It was as if their eyes were asking: "What does she mean by that?"

"Oh, please!" urged Lucinda.

"Why not?" said the man. "Never has the little one had another child to play with. We cannot keep her always to ourselves; and with this child there could be no mistake."

The light was dim on the stairs. The woman sat down on a step above Lucinda and thrust her face, close, close. It

was as if she were trying to make out the print in a book. She repeated the man's last words and smiled: "No mistake. But if you borrow her you must promise to return her safely, always. She is our very precious Trinket."

"Cross my heart!" laughed Lucinda.

There was one more new friend to come that September. Lucinda skated herself straight to him. Miss Peters had told her to take her laced shoes over to Eighth Avenue and have the cobbler there put on new toe-pieces. She had left the shoes and was skating back when the affair took place. At the corner was a fruit-stand—a very nice fruit-stand. Lucinda had often admired the gloss on the apples, the straightness of the pyramids of oranges and lemons, the good condition of the bananas. And once she had stopped and bought a Bartlett pear—they looked so nice. The Italian who owned the stand

looked nice, too. As he was an Italian, and as her parents had
gone to Italy, it had seemed right to Lucinda that she should
cultivate his acquaintance. The Bartlett pear had seemed a
good beginning but it hadn't taken her far. The man spoke
little English, Lucinda no Italian.

But on this afternoon a boy was tending the stand, a straw-
thin, undersized boy, with a mop of curly, black hair and
eyes like the picture of the young Michael Angelo that hung
in one of the classrooms at Miss Brackett's. Public school had
been let out, and the children were filling the streets on their
way home. A fattish boy and a lantern-jawed one came swag-
gering along with evil in their eyes. Lurching suddenly they
fell against the stand, and, being none too secure on its wheel
and two legs, it was shaken, spilling the fruit into the street.
The boys grabbed what fruit they could and were off down
the street, thumbing their noses back at the Italian boy.

Lucinda skated to his rescue. Silently they picked up what
fruit was left, wiped it clean, a cloth between them, replaced
each on its own pyramid. Then Lucinda lifted a face of true
compassion, and the boy nearly cried. It told how much of a
boy he was that he didn't really cry, Lucinda thought; for he
must be mad as the dickens. Ironing his lips hard against
white even teeth he said: "What can I do? My father says I
must not let them steal the fruit that way. But there are always two—and bigger than I. If I stand to protect one end,
they fall against the other. Wait until I grow big, then . . ."
He gave a dispirited shrug to his shoulders. So many years
to wait.

Lucinda was boiling with indignation: "You mean they've
done it before?"

"Three times!"

"I call that mean. Two against one and stealing, I call that mean! Jumping Jupiter, I wish Patrolman M'Gonegal had this beat! He'd lick 'em good."

Lucinda was using her best street vernacular. Like Nature in Thanatopsis she spoke a various language and used it unfailingly.

Flushed with anger and mortification, the boy smiled at Lucinda as at a miracle performed by a patron saint. "They are bad boys, cowards. They never try it when my father is here; he is big, strong. It is only when I am left in charge."

True to form Lucinda asked his name and all about his family. The family name was Coppino, his father's was Vittore; he was Tony. In her turn Lucinda dwelt heavily on the joys of being an orphan. She explained away all conscientious scruples by saying that she expected Italy was an elegant country to be living in, that her mama was undoubtedly getting well and strong there, and that both parents were probably enjoying themselves as much as she was. "Happy all 'round, you see."

Tony Coppino pressed an apple into her hand at parting. "Please take it. We are friends now. Come again."

For the two remaining afternoons of that school week Lucinda skated to Eighth Avenue and found Vittore, the father, in charge. Each afternoon she left written on the pad: "I am going around to see if my friend Tony Coppino is having any more trouble with his fruit-stand." So did the Misses Peters learn of Tony. On Saturday morning Tony was left again in charge. She was on her way to reclaim her mended shoes from the cobbler, and it was pure luck that she arrived just after the worst catastrophe that had yet occurred. A third boy had joined the original two. This time they had brought a paper bag for their loot, and almost upset the stand. Oranges, lemons, apples, tangerines—the gutter ran with them. The boys had made away with dozens, and Lucinda found Tony explaining in rapid Italian to his father what had happened. She understood him perfectly—having seen it happen once before. Tony's gestures completed the story for her: three fingers held aloft and shaken in defiance, arms rotating to convey the avalanche of fruit that fell.

When Vittore, dejected, returned to the Coppino living and storing quarters to replenish the pyramids, Lucinda accompanied him. She skated slowly, the better to explain in words of one syllable and carefully separated, how great was her sorrow. To her delight she not only made herself understood, but won a smile from Vittore's grim lips. She was equally delighted to find where they lived. In a cellar! She had never known anyone before who lived in a cellar. In the front, dark end of it the fruit was stored in crates, or barrels or hung from the ceiling in bunches. The front, light end of it was where the family lived. It opened on a sunny back-yard, which made a pleasant room, Lucinda thought. The kitchen-parlor-dining-room had two bright windows looking out on it. The garden was planted to herbs and a few flowers, and there was a heavenly smell about the whole place made up of apples, citrus fruits, garlic, and cheese. Lucinda sniffed the air, her nose wriggling like a rabbit's. What a place for goblins! She wondered if there were any there, and if Tony had seen them.

But the family were as exciting as the smells. There was Mrs. Coppino looking very smiling and bulgy. She bobbed up and down and said "Grazie—grazie," over and over. On the floor was a very small Coppino shoving itself about on its very plump and bare bottom. "Oh, it's a real bambino!" Lucinda shouted with joy. She had never seen one alive before, but her adored Cousin Lucinda Wyman had brought back pictures to her from Italy. And at this very moment, probably, her mama and papa were looking at bambinos, loose in the streets.

She threw herself, skates and all, down beside the smallest Coppino, patting its cheeks, asking Mrs. Coppino: "What is its name? Name!" Then she patted herself and said, "Lucinda." Then she patted the bambino and said again, "Name?"

Mrs. Coppino caught on. She laughed and bobbed some more and said: "Girl—Gemma."

Lucinda got up reluctantly. "Ask her if I can come back to see the bambino some other day?" she said to Vittore.

Put into Italian it brought another bobbing response. "Si—si—si!"

"She say," said Vittore, "any time come please." On the way back to the stand he managed to confide a good deal to Lucinda. Tony was a good boy, but what could he do? Soon there would be ten—twenty boys against him. He, Vittore Coppino, had to go to market, two times the week, to buy the fruit for his stand. What could he do?

Lucinda agreed with him: It was a difficult situation. She skated home slowly, much perturbed, thinking hard. But it was not until Monday and another school week had begun that a way out of the difficulty came to her. "Good-bye, Miss Peters!" she shouted upon leaving her at the curb. "I've got a perfectly elegant idea. I'm going to see if it works."

It was a complicated idea; it called for connivering, as Johanna would have said. She had no time to skate to Bryant Park that morning. She waved to Patrolman M'Gonegal and passed him at breakneck speed. She was bound for a friend made during lazy summer hours at Narragansett, where she had been allowed to run fairly free. He had a confectionery shop on Fifth Avenue at Thirty-Seventh Street, and his name was Louis Sherry. Lucinda had had many occasions to taste the excellence of his confections. Louis Sherry liked children and he was a very giving person. She was hoping now with might and main that he would be in his shop at that time in the morning.

Luck was with her. Louis Sherry was inside and busy with the day's business. He greeted Lucinda with pleasure: "And the good mama and papa—how are they?".

"Gone," said Lucinda, with a wide sweep of the hand. "I'm an orphan, a temporary orphan."

She was smiling too broadly to allow for sympathy. If she did not need sympathy what was it? Being a very keen man Louis Sherry guessed. "Let me see—it was the French curls that you always liked so much, and the chocolate nougats. Am I right? A little bag of them for consolation?"

Lucinda's smile grew. "How did you guess? They are not for myself. I want them for a bribe."

"And whom will you bribe?"

"Patrolman M'Gonegal; he has a sweet tooth."

"But don't you know it's wrong to bribe the police force? There's a law against it." The Frenchman who was born in

Vermont and was fast becoming one of the famous caterers and men of New York was trying his best to look serious. But while he was covering his amusement he was moving behind the counter, reaching for a small white paper bag with Louis Sherry in gold on it.

"Dear me!" said Lucinda. "You see, it's this way," and she proceeded to go carefully into the affairs of the Coppinos.

Louis Sherry handed over the confections with twinkling eyes. "I hope the bribe works. If you get into trouble come to me."

School over, Lucinda stood not upon the order of her going. She almost bowled Ferguson down in front of the stoop he was sweeping. Ferguson was Miss Brackett's colored man and almost as important as Miss Brackett herself. She found Patrolman M'Gonegal at the corner of the Avenue and Forty-Second Street. She beckoned him frantically to the curb and presented the bag. "From my friend, Louis Sherry."

"A friend of yours—think of that!" Patrolman M'Gonegal was impressed.

"I have a good many friends. Just now I have one suffering lots of hardships."

"As bad as that!"

"You'd be surprised how bad it is, Mr. M'Gonegal." Lucinda braced herself for the next moment. Her words came like hurrying feet: "Mr. M'Gonegal—I think you could help."

"Professional—or as a man?"

"It's this way." And again Lucinda went into the affairs of the Coppinos. She even told about the bambino named

Gemma. "I thought if you knew the policeman on their beat—Eighth Avenue and Forty-Ninth Street—he might do something."

Patrolman M'Gonegal considered: "It would be Jerry Hanlon."

"Is he nice?"

"As nice a lad as you'd find in uniform."

"There's no time to waste," said Lucinda. "I expect they are losing a dollar's worth of fruit this very afternoon."

Patrolman M'Gonegal responded like a true New York policeman of the nineties. He would make a point of seeing Jerry Hanlon that night. He would fix it up with him. After school, was it? It wouldn't take five minutes for Jerry to put the fear of God in all the boys that wanted trouble.

The next morning Lucinda was tipped off by Patrolman M'Gonegal as to arrangements. The time was to be the next day—Friday, at three sharp. Fifteen minutes ahead of that time Lucinda skated over to Eighth Avenue to make sure Tony had been left in charge of the stand, as so ordered. He was there, looking less anxious and more excited. At three sharp a youngish policeman, big, brawny, with a stout chin, appeared and greeted the two.

"I'm Jerry Hanlon; I expect the lad is Tony," and looking down at Lucinda he winked an eye. "And this would be the young lady who bribes an honest patrolman and wants to see justice done. I'm pleased to meet you, Miss." He held out a big, brawny hand and shook Lucinda almost off the pavement.

He crossed the street to a tobacco shop and took his stand inside the door, with an eye to the street. Lucinda was to skate up and down the block, as if there were nothing on her mind. When the boys appeared she was to wave her hand to Jerry Hanlon as a signal, and get fast out of the way.

School out, boys and girls began flooding the streets. Lucinda, too tense to skate, took her stand on the corner whither they were headed and watched for the fattish boy who was ringleader of this particular racket. She spotted him when he was half down the further block. She skated back and stood where Jerry Hanlon could see her. Her heart was pumping fiercely. Suppose the boys didn't do it. Suppose nothing happened! Could she ever persuade Jerry Hanlon to come back for a second time? He was supposed to be on the school corner when it emptied every afternoon. She turned to watch the end of the street; there were maneuverings going on. Five boys were lining themselves up in Indian file, hands on shoulders. They started down the street like a released torpedo, after making sure that Tony was tending the stand.

Lucinda took a long breath and waved as if all the Campbells were coming over the border. Jerry Hanlon slipped out of the tobacco shop and stood back of the wooden Indian. The boys were three-quarters towards their goal when he came into motion. He stepped off the curb into the middle of the street as the torpedo struck. Over went the stand—over went every orange and apple on it. A shower of gold and red and russet filled the street. The boys, fruit, and Jerry Hanlon were messed up together. One boy got an upper cut that laid him flat; one got a kick in the shins that sent him sprawling; two Jerry Hanlon grabbed by an ear each. Lucinda butted, head-on, into the last like a rambunctious goat. He went down hard before the onslaught, Lucinda straddling on top of him. She sat there while Jerry Hanlon put the fear of God and the law in all five, impartially.

He called to Tony, had him take out his book from his pocket, and write down the names, where the boys lived, what their fathers did. He told them, jerking the two boys he held by the ears, glowering at them all, that if they so much as swiped one orange again or any boy started monkeyshining 'round the stand, he'd have them all up in the precinct court as quick as a cat could wink her eye.

The five went their separate ways; if a steam roller had gone over them they could have looked no more crushed. Bystanders hooted them out of sight while they helped Tony, Lucinda, and Jerry Hanlon to recover the fruit. Much was ruined, but wasn't it worth it? Lucinda stayed to wipe clean what could be put back on the stand. "Are we chortling?" she asked Tony. "Are we beamish? Were they slithy toves and did we go for them snicker-snack!"

Miss Peters, coming home early that afternoon, found written on the pad:

I am skating 'round to Tony's stand. Something's going to happen. If it happens right I shall be coming home with banners waving. O frabjous day!

September 14th, 189—

I have had a hard time deciding about churches. Mama said—church or Sunday School, but she didn't say which church. You see we changed from Dr. Collyer's a couple of years ago because Aunt Emily went Swedenborgian and dragged mama with her. Mama dragged me. It was all because of Heaven and Hell. It seemed that Mr. Swedenborg knew more about it than anybody else, having peaked through the keyhole or something. Luckily he's dead or Aunt Emily wouldn't be leaving him alone for a moment. She always has to know about everything.

But I think you ought to stay in the church you were christened in. And Dr. Collyer christened me. So I've gone back to the Church of The Messiah—and there I stick.

Saturday Aunt Emily had to stir things up because I wasn't in her Sunday School. She'll keep it up until mama comes home but I'm not going to weaken. I was very polite about it, outside; but inside I boiled.

September 22nd.

Went to church. Skated there. It was pokey to have to go on the hoof before. The church has a nice Sexton; he says he remembers the day I was christened there, but that is what you'd call poetic something or other, I guess, for I was christened at home. I don't remember it but I've heard about it enough times to know that Dr. Collyer came up for Sunday dinner and did it in the afternoon—all relatives present. Of course, I was in swaddling clothes—I guess that's the Bible word for diapers—more elegant though. I talked over the skate matter with the Sexton. He said Lucinda it would be as much as my job is worth if you took skates into the pew. But if you come early and leave late, after the fashionables, I'll keep them for you in the vestry closet. Very pleasantly settled. So early I come. He's traveled a lot. It makes interesting conversation when you get old. I guess he likes my coming this way. He says standing an hour in a stiff collar gives him giraffe's neck. I don't know whether I ought to tell Miss Peters about skating to church. I go in my best bib-and-tucker. She might think it wasn't suitable.

I guess I'll let her find it out.

CHAPTER III

AN EXCITING MEETING
WITH MR. WILLIAM SHAKESPEARE

FOR ten years life for Lucinda had been systematic. At
almost any waking hour of it she could have pointed
finger at the clock and said: It is time for this or that. Aunt
Emily had brought Lucinda's mother up on System, Duty,
and Discipline; these were for Aunt Emily the three Rs
of living. After Lucinda's mother had struggled somewhat
against them for half a lifetime she still had not weakened
enough to make the slow running of days always pleasant; ac-
cording to Lucinda's idea of what it might be.

Life behind the brownstone front, two flights up and beyond, was delightfully higgledy-piggledy as to System; and
Duty and Discipline had become pale, thin creatures that no
longer cast shadows except on Saturdays—from four o'clock
on. Saturday was dedicated to Aunt Emily and sewing. Lucinda buttoned up her fortitude and best manners, when she
buttoned her best pinafore, made of white French lawn,
Hamburg edging, and sleeveless. It was a step up in the world
above the pongee. Pinafores were accountable to Aunt Emily.
She had started her own daughters in them and had thumb-
screwed Lucinda's mother into thinking they were what
every growing girl should wear.

There had been two faultless, best-mannered Saturdays
since Lucinda had joined the orphanage. There had been no
tantrums; and Lucinda had carried up to her third Saturday
some hope and a certain amount of thanksgiving that everything had gone so well. She had grown old enough to realize
that combat with Aunt Emily ended in defeat for her. For
two afternoons—four to six—she had sat very properly on her
chair, legs dangling, had tried to take small, neat stitches, and
had kept her mouth safely shut while Aunt Emily had repeated by word of mouth everything—and a little more—that
she had written in that letter that had arrived nearly in time
to upset Lucinda's year.

Meekly Lucinda had bent to Aunt Emily's command that
she should not skate there on Saturdays. She should come
walking, like a little lady. Twice Lucinda had managed it
without too much rebellion; and had arrived in a reasonable
frame of mind. But the third Saturday was a day for out-of-
doors, a day for free movement and shouting, a day to spend

with a boy. Tony, having the last of the afternoon free, had asked her to spend it in the Park—had even invited her to one ride on the swan boats. She had wanted terribly to go.

Having gotten off to none too good a start and needing something to bolster her feelings, Lucinda conceived the delightful new game of really arriving at Aunt Emily's like a lady. She fell behind several ladies, dropping them when their direction changed from hers; and she imitated each detail of posture and walk. She had waddled behind a fat woman, she had strutted behind a proud one. Now as she approached Aunt Emily's, she fell in behind a timid, and a nervous one, who minced in walking, and darted furtive glances at houses, persons, and vehicles that she passed. By this time Lucinda was enjoying the game; it had taken her mind off her disappointment. She was working into her best form as she reached the stoop. Elation carried her on for a few yards; then she turned, ran back, and climbed the stone steps, two at a time.

She had worked off much energy; she was prepared to be a model child, to take pains with her sewing and answer Aunt Emily properly: "Yes, Aunt Emily."——"No, Aunt Emily."——"If you wish, Aunt Emily." Her lips were moving on the words silently, by way of reminder. There was no reason to believe that all would not have continued as on the previous Saturdays.

But Aunt Emily had been standing behind the Brussels net curtain; she had watched well Lucinda's deportment up her street, straight to her front door. It is best to remember the dead kindly—or as kindly as one can. So I will not describe how Aunt Emily opened the door, herself, for Lucinda, how she looked, how she held a frozen, thin-lipped silence until Lucinda had taken her chair and opened her sewing basket. I will not repeat the things Aunt Emily said then, in one of the worst moments Lucinda had ever seen her.

Lucinda held her tongue by the simple device of biting it between her teeth. It caused a thrust-out look to the lips; and for this she was reprimanded. "Lucinda, why are you making a face like that? Are you making it *deliberately?*"

"Not exactly, Aunt Emily."

"What do you mean by not exactly?"

"I mean just that!" Lucinda's voice was jerking out the words and beginning to fling them at Aunt Emily. Inside she was thinking: Why can't she leave me alone until I get hold of myself?

"Have you anything else to say, Lucinda?"

She knew what that called for. She was expected to say

how very sorry she was—how wholly, completely ashamed of herself—and that she would never do it again. She was to throw herself upon Aunt Emily's charity and allow Aunt Emily to forgive her.

Being Lucinda, she could not manage so much humility. She sat up straighter; she gripped one dangling foot with another. She looked very straight and unashamed and said: "Well, you asked me to come—looking like a lady. Aunt Emily, I'm not one. We both know that. So I just copied ladies—going my way; and I did it the best I could." Remembering with what abandoned delight she had done it she couldn't suppress a giggle. It was out and away before she knew it.

Aunt Emily was outraged. "Lucinda, you will sew for the next half hour without speaking. I cannot have you setting my own good little girls such an example of impertinence."

So Lucinda sat. She glowered at the four docile daughters —Frances, Virginia, Sybil, and Agatha. Left to themselves, beyond the reach of Aunt Emily's invading eye, Lucinda could have a fairly good time with them. But in Aunt Emily's presence they became prigs. As her eyes traveled from face to face she could see on each a holier-than-thou look. She dug her needle viciously into the petticoat she was supposed to be making. She believed the devil must have invented a needle. From the moment you first learned to thread one, and knot the thread, it had you plagued to death. She hated—hated— hated sewing—this kind of sewing!

For the next five minutes the needle was yanked and pushed, in and out. Then it became unthreaded and had to be threaded again. Then the thread knotted and broke, and a beginning had to be made all over. If anybody had scuffled her feet along the carpet and given Lucinda a spark, it would have set her off like a package of firecrackers.

And somebody did. Aunt Emily. She saw the jerks and the yanks and she approached Lucinda with a forbidding eye. "You'll never learn to sew nicely that way. You must learn to control your temper. Look at my little girls. How patient they are. You're so good at imitating others, you might try imitating them."

The whole Fourth of July went off inside of Lucinda. Her sewing basket, scissors, thimble, work went across the room. She bounced to her feet, her eyes blazing forth some of the inward fire. "I know I don't sew nicely—I'll never, never sew nicely. I wish I was in heaven and you and your everlasting sewing in hell, Aunt Emily!" Lucinda did not intend this to be the damning thing it sounded. She had wanted to place Aunt Emily and herself as far apart as possible.

A silence so horrible followed that Lucinda wished herself dead-and-be-done-with. Out of that silence rose Aunt Emily's voice. "I cannot allow you to stay and have supper. Get on your things. Katie will take you back to your boarding house."

But Aunt Emily reckoned without fate. In the doorway stood Uncle Earle. He had heard everything. He gave Lucinda the impression of laughing although not a muscle in his face moved. His eyes were very serious, his voice very solemn. "If Lucinda is too wicked to stay in the parlor, I suggest that she come to the library and have supper there. Her temper will have no effect either on me or the books. Come along, Lucinda."

He drew her to the doorway and stood there long enough

to make a second remark: "You must remember, Emily, that all children are not turned out the same, like button-molds, or like your own little gazelles."

The library was Uncle Earle's own room; hardly anyone else ever came there. It smelt of tobacco and worn leather and books. It was the haven or heaven that Lucinda had wished herself in a moment before. The chairs were deep and embracing; pitted all over with buttons. Lucinda selected hers and almost disappeared into it while Uncle Earle looked over the bookshelves. At last he said, "Ever met William Shakespeare, Lucinda?"

"I haven't, but I've heard about him. Quotations, you know, every morning at Brackett's. You get to hear about a lot of people that way—but never to know them."

"Well, it's time you knew your Shakespeare. We'll try *The Tempest*. You'll meet up with some of your own kind in it. It all happened on an enchanted island that never existed on the farthest sea. It makes enchanted reading."

He took down a book, took his chair opposite, opened the book and began the cast of characters: "Alonso, King of Naples, Sebastian, his brother, Prospero, the right Duke of Milan. Mark that, Lucinda, the *right* duke. Antonio, the false duke, Ferdinand, son to the king . . . Ariel, an airy Spirit."

"Does that mean a fairy?"

"An elemental. They are much the same. Ariel—Puck—you'll dote on the fairies Mr. Shakespeare has caught and held for children of all time. Better than sewing, eh, Lucinda?" Uncle Earle looked up over his glasses and winked solemnly. Everything about him was big—even his wink. His face was set about with reddish chop whiskers, with room in the middle to kiss without scrubbing. But it was his eyes Lucinda liked best. They were as blue as dust flowers along the sea road at Narragansett; and they told you things that the lips left unsaid, that is, if you were a little girl and your name was Lucinda.

Uncle Earle read *The Tempest* into a slow-gathering dusk. Only once did he stop, to ring for Lucinda's supper. "I can feel your Aunt Emily's disapproval rising up through the floor. She would have made a good Roman centurion." He took Lucinda's chin in his big, finely shaped hand and waggled her head, asking: "Shall we on with the play?"

They on-ed. Katie brought up the supper tray and Lucinda noted with satisfaction that Aunt Emily had not scrimped on her. There were croissants from Purssell's, creamed chicken, charlotte-russe, and cocoa. Came seven o'clock and *The Tempest* was over. It was time for Uncle Earle to go down for his dinner. Lucinda bore her feet to earth, or rather to the library carpet, with reluctance. She clasped Uncle Earle around the middle and prodded a fierce head into his stomach; she was trying to convey something of her joy and gratitude, having no words lovely enough. She would have to hunt through the dictionary as soon as she got home to find new ones to use for Mr. William Shakespeare.

"Here, take it along." Uncle Earle thrust the small red book into her hands. "You'll be wanting to read it all over again by yourself. And what about going home?"

"I'll go alone. Please, Uncle Earle! I'll go quick as a jackrabbit."

Together they conspired to get Lucinda out of the house without being discovered. Into the late, keen twilight of that

September day Lucinda went in a state of pure rapture. She wished she had her roller skates—thereby gaining a motion free, flying, that would give vent to some of the emotion within. She thrust hands deep into her reefer pockets and took to a jog-trot. Her head was tilted upwards that the rows of brownstone houses might be obliterated, that she might see overhead only that ribbon of sky which undoubtedly was unfurled over Prospero's magic island.

So would she have run amuck several times had not passersby given her good thoroughfare. "Ariel, I love you—I adore you." She was shouting it in whispers as she took the curb.

"Hey, you, there!" a boy driving a delivery wagon, was turning the corner. He reined in his horse just in time to avoid running down Lucinda. "Say—what's the matter with your head? Can't you look where you walk?"

"I'm looking all right." Lucinda walked under the horse's nose and turned to grin back at the boy, "You see, I'm not walking where you think I am; I'm walking on those yellow sands with Ariel."

"You're crazy as a bed-bug," said the boy.

Back with Miss Peters and Miss Nettie, she did full justice to the afternoon, generous alike to her humiliation and her joy. "I expect you had better punish me. You see, Aunt Emily tried her best; but this time Uncle Earle interfered. I was terrible, but Aunt Emily was funny. She looked exactly like the Queen of Hearts about to say: 'Off with her head!'"

Miss Peters, knowing Aunt Emily too well, was not inclined towards punishment. She rebuked Lucinda gravely and urged better behavior in the future. "I guess there won't be any future." Lucinda was not quite certain whether to be glad because the sewing was over and done with or sorry because she would lose the good suppers and Uncle Earle. "Aunt Emily'll never have me there again. I'm too bad an example for the gazelles. Isn't that a heavenly name for them? Uncle Earle invented it. But at least never again will I have to sew there. I'm just not the sort to sit on a cushion and sew a fine seam."

But the next moment she had forgotten her abhorrence of sewing. She was catching at an idea and sharing it abundantly. Uncle Earle had told her it was the custom in Mr. Shakespeare's time to give a play at Twelfth Night. Could there be a better play than *The Tempest*? She went into the work-room and staggered out with the theatre, sat down on the floor with it, and talked in an unbroken stream. She showed her accumulation of doll-actors; explained the theatre that was made out of a stout wooden box, with a back that dropped down on hinges like the lid of a desk. There were grooves at the bottom on which to run scenery; there were slits chiseled out at the sides, front and back, through which the actors made their entrances and exits. Lucinda had conceived the idea of such a theatre when she was six and had been taken for the first time inside of one. The D'Oyly Carte Company had brought over *The Mikado* from England. The next year a Drury Lane Pantomime had come over; and Lucinda became more convinced than ever that she must have a theatre of her own. Later she saw *Little Lord Fauntleroy;* but that added nothing to her enthusiasms. To her oldest brother, at home for his Christmas holidays, Lucinda spoke her dream aloud; and he had made the bare bones of it. She had written two plays, made out of Robin Hood from Howard Pyle's book, and from one of Johanna's Irish fairy-tales, the one called Peter, the Humpy. She and Johanna had spent a whole winter making Sherwood Forest and jerkins of Lincoln green. There was no time to lose if she was to have *The Tempest* ready by Twelfth Night.

Her tongue had run on long past her bed-time; Miss Peters bridled it with difficulty. "But it's such fun talking. Isn't it an elegant idea? Can't I stay up ten minutes more—five minutes? Tomorrow's Sunday. Will you help me with the costumes, Miss Nettie? There'll be so many different kinds. What do you think Caliban ought to wear?"

By the time that she had folded her clothes on the chair, said her prayers, put out the light, plunged, flapping, to the folding bed, and drawn blankets to chin, her fancy was flaming high. She would ask everybody to come. Tony would help; you always needed a boy for such things. What fun telling everybody! She would begin tomorrow. No time to waste; it wouldn't do to have anybody make another engagement. She would say to all her friends: "I'm giving a performance of Mr. Shakespeare's *Tempest* on Twelfth Night; and you're invited!" Wouldn't that make their eyes pop! Wouldn't they wonder what sort of performance it would be! And wouldn't it be a magnificent surprise when they found out? Sleep was close at hand when she came to her final inspiration. "I'll invite Uncle Earle, but I won't ask Aunt Emily and the gazelles. We'll keep it a secret from them."

For days her joy mounted. She had to tell everybody about it: Patrolman M'Gonegal, Tony, even Miss Brackett. She forgot the terrible person Miss Brackett was, remembering only the wonderful, and invited her, "I would like ever so much to have you come. Have you ever seen *The Tempest* done on a table?"

Miss Brackett had to agree that she never had. She seemed pleased to be invited.

Lucinda took an afternoon to skate down to the Gedney House to tell her friends there. She found Mrs. Caldwell in her room. Pygmalion was dozing in his basket; but was up in a whisk, with a volley of barks and a variety of contortions to welcome her. Lucinda was as expressive in her way as the tiny black and tan.

"I declare I've been homesick for Piggy—and never knew it! Can't I take him out for a walk—I mean a skate? He'll love it, truly, Mrs. Caldwell. And when I get back I'll tell you all about my performance of Mr. Shakespeare's *Tempest* I'm going to have on Twelfth Night. I might even have two performances. One could be here at the hotel—if Mr. Spindler liked the idea."

Mr. Spindler did; Mrs. Spindler more. They would have it in their own apartment on the day following; and would invite special guests.

She greeted Charlie, the doorman; and had a word with Buttons as he was going to answer a bell. In one running-away sentence he had told her the news of the hotel. "We've got two grand new families here. Aleda is almost as nice as you are. Her grandmother and grandfather are actors. Good ones, you bet; and she goes to every matinée. The other's a lady—a sort of heathen Chinee. Got a suite—they have—all fixed up like a museum. And it's a nickel or a dime every time she rings. She rings plenty, too."

Lucinda resumed her skates; and with Pygmalion on his leash they celebrated the peak of Lucinda's joy on Broadway. It took on something of the nature of a riot. Pygmalion was accustomed only to sedate walks with his mistress; but with Lucinda on skates—here was an event. Other dogs joined in, other children on skates, in free, joyous vagabondage. Lucinda yipped; Pygmalion yapped; the others expressed themselves as they chose. Mr. Gilligan passed with a fare and waved his whip until he was out of sight.

She was dog-tired, as Pygmalion had been, when she came in at five-thirty and threw herself bodily upon Miss Nettie. "I'm just too happy to live. Could I have a bath before supper and eat in bed with the cutting table close beside it?"

She sang as she undressed; as the water ran against the tin of the tub it made a pleasant accompaniment. She brought to her supper a face scrubbed and glowing like a harvest moon. For the first time she begged for company: "Just a few minutes—before you go down to dinner. Isn't it elegant not to have tantrums any more! I guess half of it is because you don't expect them; and the other half is roller skates. They use up a lot of energy and iron out a lot of feelings. Like Mrs. Winslow's Soothing Syrup—they ought to be called 'the mother's friend.' "

Lucinda went to sleep that night thinking she would be needing a good deal of money. Her allowance was one dollar a week, dealt out by Miss Peters. Fifty cents for car-fare to and from school, but saved every day but a rainy day. Five cents for the plate—Sundays—and the rest for sundries. Having spent little, Lucinda found herself in October with a full purse, feeling terribly Jay Gouldish. But even a full purse could be emptied.

Out of school the next noon, she wasted no time with shin-annigins. She bolted her dinner; tore up to the parlor; took off her pinafore; wadded it into a ball and kicked it into her wardrobe. She was going to be her own Lucinda for the rest of the day and wear nothing and do nothing that marked her otherwise. She had on her Scotch plaid gingham and it did look nice. She put on Sunday shoes; they had kid bottoms and cloth tops and they buttoned snug and high. Her legs looked nice in them; if only they didn't have to go into under-drawers, long bulgy ones, the last of the month.

Before going to sleep the night before she had written in her diary a list of those things that she would need for *The Tempest*. Now she unlocked her desk and read it again to be sure she remembered everything. Reefer on, the elastic band of her sailor snapped under her chin, skates buckled and dangling, she closed the door upon her going and took the stairs up to the third floor. She was going to borrow Trinket.

She found the Browdowskis home at the back and knocked, waited, knocked again. When the door opened it was only a crack; the not-so-tall woman who was Trinket's mother put her face to the crack and looked startled. Then she opened the door a little wider but held her body against it as if she were hiding something. Not so long afterwards, Lucinda was to discover what it was. Instinct prodded her into caution. She mustn't say the wrong thing; she mustn't ask to come in. Instead she smiled eagerly: "I'm Lucinda Wyman, one flight down. You remember? You said I could borrow Trinket and I want her today."

There was hesitation but Lucinda went exuberantly on, trusting her instinct. She told about her theatre, about *The Tempest*. Now she was going over to Sixth Avenue, to Jenkins and the toy-shop—the lovely toy-shop. There would be such pretty things to see there; she thought Trinket would love them. And she promised to hold Trinket's hand all the way and be careful about curbs.

Consent came at last. "Yes, I think she can go. Trinket's father isn't here, but I think he would want her to go. Please wait downstairs. I'll have her ready in a minute."

Lucinda waited by the front door. They came, Mrs. Browdowski leading Trinket. As always, the tiny girl's face was very solemn but there was a shining expectancy there as well. Rather awed, Lucinda received Trinket's hand from her mother's. "Doll's size, isn't it? I feel just as if I were taking my biggest French doll for a walk; only nicer—much nicer."

On the lowest step she put on her skates and then away they went, slowly but with suppressed excitement. Trinket tripped to Lucinda's moderated swing. Lucinda talked; Trinket listened. At Jenkins' Lucinda bought cardboard and crayons, paints, especially silver, and two new brushes.

Jenkins was only an incident, the toy-shop was an event. Trinket had plainly never been in a toy-shop before and it cast a spell upon her which Lucinda watched with growing delight. She lifted the tiny girl up to see the marvels on the higher shelves, and was amazed to find how light she was. "Why, you only weigh one feather, Trinket. The wind will blow you into the sky some day if we don't watch out."

They lost themselves in an hour of enchantment. The shop person in charge knew Lucinda and let them take their time. There was a Prospero and a false duke, a king and a Ferdinand to buy; and none was to be had with a beard. Lucinda was shocked at the extreme youth of all of them. "Don't dolls ever grow old? And why not? Well, I wish they'd begin to make some nice old men and women dolls. I need them in my specialty."

"What is it?" asked the shop person.

"The theatre," and Lucinda said it in her grandest manner.

What delighted Trinket most was not the dolls but the little kid ankle-ties on the dolls—pink, white, and blue. She touched them with a quivering forefinger and said: "Pretty, so pretty." It was almost the only words she spoke through that whole afternoon.

There was a boxful of tiny dolls in different-colored dresses and tiny kid slippers. They gave Lucinda an idea. She left Trinket, to whisper an aside to the shop person: "How much?"

"Fifty cents apiece."

Fifty cents came out of the purse and Lucinda hurried back and artfully inquired. "See, Trinket, these little dollies have slippers, too. Aren't they pretty?" And when Trinket agreed, "What color do you think is the prettiest?"

The tiny girl ran her finger up and down the box several times; at last it came to rest on the doll dressed in red, with white slippers and sash. Lucinda beckoned to the shop person. "Wouldn't you like to have this little girl take a doll home with her?"

The shop person thought it would be a splendid idea, cut the string at the back of the box, and pulled out the doll in red. The hands that were doll's size reached for it and clasped it under Trinket's own chin. Lucinda nodded vigorously to the look of question on the still solemn face: "Yes, it's yours—your very own—to take home and keep."

Inside she felt a riot. It worked with Trinket just as it had worked when she was Trinket's size and her adored Uncle Earle had taken her to a toy-shop and she had been given the little red cart she wanted in the same mysterious way.

Back in the Misses Peters' parlour Lucinda took off Trinket's things and then her own. She drew up a rocking-chair, lifted Trinket to her lap, and felt with astonishment the little body that weighed only one feather nestle to hers. There was not length enough to Lucinda to hold the long sigh of contentment she gave; it snapped off when it got to the bottom of her boots. She had never had a little girl to play with and she had wanted one sorely. She was the youngest—no baby had ever followed her in the families of aunts or uncles. She never expected to own—half or quarter—anything as darling as Trinket. It was wonderful—too wonderful!

She looked down at the small, rapt face turned up to hers for the moment in complete surrender, then back to the precious doll she held in her lap. "I tell you what we'll do," said Lucinda. "We'll sing your dolly to sleep. We'll sing: 'Froggy would a-wooing go.' That's the song I used to like best when I was only as big as a pint-pot." So Lucinda sang:

FROGGY WOULD A-WOOING GO

"Froggy would a-wooing go,
    Heigh-O, said Rowley;
Froggy would a-wooing go
Whether his mother would let him or no;
With a rolly, polly, gammon and spinach—
    Heigh-O, said Rowley;

So off he went with his opera hat;
    Heigh-O, said Rowley;
So off he went with his opera hat,
And on the way he met with a rat;
With a rolly, polly, gammon and spinach—
    Heigh-O, said Rowley."

A few days later Lucinda went up again to borrow Trinket and wrote of it in her diary.

October 1st, 189—

Things I am going to need for Mr. Shakespeare's Tempest
White cardboard for scenery. More paints. Crayons.
I'll have to find some rocks for Prospero's cave.
A ship—being wrecked. Yellow sands.

1 Prospero—the right duke. If I can't find a doll with a beard
   I'll have to buy false hair.
2 Alonso, the king—maybe he had better be bearded.
3 Antonio—the false duke. No, I think I'll leave him out;
   he's not too important. But maybe he is.
4 Ferdinand—Miranda's beau. I must have him handsome.
5 Mariners—that means sailors. Two will do.
6 Caliban—a mishapen monster. I'm afraid he can't be
   bought.

Ariel—an airy Spirit. I don't need to buy one, I have a perfect
Ariel.

Pieces of silks, velvets, satins and such for costumes. I think
Miss Nettie will help me out with scraps from her customers.

October 4th, 189—

I wish mama was here, she'd know what to do.
I have made a terrible discovery about Trinket and her parents. It rained all day so I went up again to borrow Trinket.
Miss Nettie had cut out costumes for Prospero and the King
and I was going to sew them. I like that kind of sewing when
there's no one around to say Lucinda watch your stitches.
When I went up to get Trinket no one was there but her (or

is it she) anyway, she was there alone and she opened the door and pulled me straight inside the room. It was awful—just the bare bones of a room. In the corner was a wooden packing box made into a kind of cupboard, dishes and little packages of food inside and on top a gas contraption to cook on. There was a bureau, a bed, a crib and a piece of faded calico hung along one wall. I guess they hung their clothes back of it. Nothing else, nothing nice! They must be so poor it hurts. I didn't think Mrs. B. (I don't know how to spell her name) would want to find me in the room so I took Trinket down with me and ran up afterwards and pinned a note on the door to say where she was. Trinket brought her dolly down and I said I would make her another dress and let her be a nymph in the play.

Trinket's mother let me keep her for supper. We used the doll's tea set and I made Trinket laugh.

I've made up my mind to say nothing to Miss P. or Miss N. about what I saw upstairs. Mama says there are times when it's kinder not to tell things. But I am going to have Trinket down often for supper—every other night, perhaps. I guess I am catching the interfering habit from Aunt Emily. Maybe I am like her. Whew!

CHAPTER IV

MOSTLY RUBBISH

THE next day was Saturday. It was no longer forsworn
to Aunt Emily. Tony had an elegant idea of what could
be done with it. "Have you ever roasted potatoes in a tin
can?" he asked Lucinda as she skated around a peaceful corner on Eighth Avenue early in the morning. "Look, it is a day
given to us by the good Maria."

Lucinda's imagination needed no prodding. "You mean
a picnic. Elegant! On the shore in Maine we have the best
picnics. We scoop out the sand, fill the hole with driftwood,
and when it burns down to charcoal we pile in lobsters, chick-
en, potatoes, corn—anything almost. Then we cover it with
seaweed and stones and when it's done—golly!"

"The potatoes—they are golly, too!" Tony was not to be outdone.

"I wish we could have a New York picnic."

"We can. Often I do it."

"Where?"

"Almost anywhere. An empty lot is good. The Park . . ."

"Elegant. We'll do it now! We'll hunt stones and things for scenery. I'll bring Mr. Shakespeare along and read you the whole play. Where do we get the cans and potatoes?"

Tony patted his chest with pride. "In our cellar we got everything. We even got charcoal. As soon as my papa gets back from market—one hour—one hour and a half—I will have everything ready."

"I'll get the rest." Lucinda was all of a dither. She arrived in the Misses Peters' parlor breathless and demanded of Miss Peters if she could go on a picnic with Tony Coppino. "It's just a picnic; the same as we have in Maine only in an empty lot instead of on the shore. More exciting. Don't you see?"

Miss Peters did, but not with pleasure. She had made it a point to go around to the fruit-stand on Eighth Avenue and take her own measurements of Tony and his father. She had been satisfied with what she had seen; they were simple, honest Italians, minding their own business. But here was Lucinda asking for a picnic in an empty lot. She knew that a Lucinda, cooped up, forbidden this and that, was bound to be a restless, dissatisfied Lucinda. Nature had succeeded in pumping her full of ideas and energy which ran amuck when not worked off. But where would it end? Her voice dragged as with the weight of stone: "Honestly, Lucinda, what do you think your mother would think of picnics in empty lots!"

"Just one picnic and one lot. We'll choose a nice, tidy one."

"But it isn't the place for little girls to be."

"Tony isn't a girl. Tony'll look after me if I need looking after. We'll be as safe as snifflebugs."

"He couldn't look after his stand very well."

"Then I'll look after him," Lucinda exploded with laughter. "Just what do you think would happen to us, Miss Peters? Think of all of the plagues of Egypt; there isn't one likely to overtake us in an empty lot."

Miss Peters was laughing, now. "I guess you're on the lap of the gods this year," she said, and Lucinda wondered what she meant. But she helped her make sandwiches and put salt and butter in little packages. Black Sarah gave her four cupcakes, frosted with chocolate. Tony had no skates so Lucinda loaned him one of hers. "We'll go single-legged," she said, "we can cover the ground about as fast."

They did. Up Broadway they went to the Park and skirted it, block after block. Over Tony's shoulders hung the cans, front and back, fastened with hoops of wire. In one hand he carried a sack of charcoal, in the other a sack of fruit. Lucinda swung her one bundle and her tongue, with Mr. Shakespeare in the reefer pocket. They passed Hunter's Gate. They passed Mariner's Gate and found an empty lot just beyond. Not much rubbish and quite spic and span in one corner where there was a hump of gray, granite rock and a tree of sorts.

In a business-like way, as one who knew what he was doing, Tony set to work. There were holes in the covers of the cans; about each a wire had been twisted tight with a couple of feet free and a loop in each end. He filled the cans quarter full of charcoal, lighted it, screwed on the tops and gave one to Lucinda. "Swing it hard, till you get it to burn."

Here was a new magic that enthralled her. A few minutes and Tony lifted the covers and showed the charcoal glowing red. He put into each can two potatoes, screwed down the covers again and said: "Swing and wait. Potatoes cook better when not too much swing."

The boy and girl sat on the granite hump and talked. Little by little, innermost, secret things came to the surface of their minds. They skimmed these off and shared them. Tony had great ambitions to use his hands for beauty. "I see things first that are not ugly," he put it, "like a copper bowl of fruit, like flowers in a window, like swans against the green water of the pond. I think I can make all these things so other people can see them, too."

"Why don't you?" asked Lucinda.

"I have nothing to make with, and no place to make. Always there are babies in our home to turn things upside down." He laughed without rancor.

"You mean you need paints and brushes—that stuff. Well, I've got them—plenty. And there's Miss Peters' parlor— plenty of room there. Why, you can make the scenery for *The Tempest*. Listen!" Out of the reefer pocket came Mr. Shakespeare. Lucinda wished she could read it as had Uncle Earle. But she picked her favorite scenes, explaining between them. She noticed with a quickening eye how the imagery caught at Tony's spirit. He sucked in his breath at this new discovery of beauty in words.

When she came to Caliban she spoke her fear for him:

"You can't buy a Caliban in a toy-shop. Where will we find one?"

Tony patted his pocket, drew out an old jack-knife with one blade. "Here—you shall see. I make all kinds of toys for the babies. I make your Caliban, out of wood or a good warty potato."

From the cans were coming the pleasant smell of roasting potatoes. It was time to spread the picnic. Lucinda opened her bundle; Tony ripped the paper sack that held the fruit and spread it flat to make a platter. There were bananas and oranges, and for Lucinda a Bartlett pear. "My papa remember how you like them."

It was a perfect picnic day; no flies to crawl over the food, no insects to fly in the butter. There was flooding of sunshine, but the air had a knife's edge to it; you could feel winter on its way. "I'll build a fire," said Tony. He pointed to the ground below the cover of the rock. "It will burn well there; it will warm fingers and toes; the potatoes will warm the middle of us." He set about gathering dried weeds, stray papers, pieces from a broken barrel.

The sound of jangling bells caused both children to look towards the street. A man on the seat of a cart full of rubbish was walking his horse close to the curb. A good smell in the wind brought him to his feet and he looked straight over the edge of the lot to where the children had spread their picnic and lighted their fire. He stopped the cart, waved a hand to them, jumped down and wrapped the reins about a tree, knotted them and crossed the road to the lot.

Lucinda grabbed Tony's hand. "I simply don't feel comfortable inside. Suppose— —" But she did not dare to say it.

The man was pulling himself up on the granite hump. The closer he got the more disreputable he looked. His face was covered with stubble growth, his clothes were the pick of rag-heaps. He was dirty. The children could take to their heels and leave their picnic behind; they could stay and meet him—man to man. They stayed.

He was crossing the hump towards them when he must have seen something in their faces to bring him to a full stop. He smiled, and over the smile his eyes showed friendly, like a dog's. Smile and eyes together dispelled their fear. Here was kin to the earth, the sun, the creatures; someone benignly elemental. Lucinda found herself grinning; Tony stood watchful, still uncertain.

The man beat his hands together as if they were cold. He knelt on the rock and held them over the fire below. He did not look at either of them when he spoke: "Well, young lady, young gentleman, I'm old Rags-an'-Bottles. Often I comes here a-noonin'; but it ain't often I finds company." He turned, looked at each, smelled the air like a hungry terrier. His smile grew. "Roasted potatoes, dang 'em, or I'm a zebra."

This plainly called for an invitation to lunch; but the girl and boy looked at each other with consternation. There were four of everything—potatoes, cup-cakes, bananas, meat sandwiches, jelly sandwiches. Lucinda was too good at arithmetic not to know that four divided by three didn't work. From each other they looked to old Rags-an'-Bottles. He was sitting now, dangling his feet down beside the fire, and his eyes were feasting on the food spread on Lucinda's white napkin and Tony's brown paper. He looked up and caught their eyes upon him. "If I was asked now to stay and try my snags o' teeth in this what you'd call a banquet; why, stay I would."

They invited him in their best manner. Four was divided by three, with the one left over going by common consent to old Rags-an'-Bottles. Even the Bartlett pear was offered and accepted. But Lucinda felt it was his by right of that law, Give that ye may receive. What stories he had to give in turn! He made his daily round of collecting rags and rubbish the most romantic adventure life could hold. He told of fine houses, of strange people; he told of thieves and of murder done; he told of wharves and sailors coming in on ships that had touched the farthest point of the earth, bringing with them parrots, monkeys, little strange creatures he could not name.

He, too, lived in a cellar, but his was all cellar. By the light of a candle he picked over his rags, sorted his takings for the day. As rags and rubbish they started, as rags and rubbish they often ended. But not always! There was luck to be reckoned with. "You can never tell, young lady, young gentleman, what will turn up."

Just like Mr. Micawber, thought Lucinda in a kind of wonder.

"That's what keeps me at it, an' me goin' on seventy. It's expectin' an' huntin' an' findin'. Some I finds in pockets; some I finds stuck or caught careless-like; some I finds sewed in linin's. That surprises you, young lady. But I'm tellin' what I knows. Often there ain't no pockets, and then again you dig in a hand and close hard on two bits. Other times, it's a wad o' green-uns. I've pulled 'em out with a ten marked on 'em. Be-elzebub!"

He made Lucinda want to own a cart with bells strung over the top to jangle pleasantly at every step of a horse named Minnie. Think of it—a whole city to go a-rubbishing in! With luck there might be goblins in the cellar; and hidden treasure every other day, hunted for by the light of one candle. Old Rags-an'-Bottles went on pulling priceless romance out of the past: "Time I've had a queen's brooch in my hand, caught in a bit of lace, grimy as an old cobweb; time I've pulled out a pearl pin from a cravat in ribbons. Look at this 'ere hand. It's held diamonds, rubies!" He turned over and over his gnarled, dirty hand and looked at it in puzzled wonder, as if, somehow it could work miracles.

Lucinda, having almost seen the jewels there, was as puzzled as old Rags-an'-Bottles at their sudden vanishing. "Oh, dear, you must be a very rich man by now," she ventured.

"Not rich exactly, but comin' on, young lady."

It was the full noon of the day. What wind had stirred was gone; the sun shone down with almost summer strength and for a moment there arose from the close neighborhood of old Rags-an'-Bottles a shocking smell of the dirt and discard of the city. Lucinda, having a cautious nose, backed farther away, her nostrils quivering like a rabbit's. Perhaps she wouldn't care much about going a-rubbishing. Perhaps it would be better to leave it to others who carried no nose for smells, no objection to dirt.

The children gathered up their things while old Rags-an'-Bottles dozed in the sun. They thought him hard asleep and would have stolen off without waking him, but he cocked an eye at them and said, as they were going, "How about next Saturday, the day bein' fine? I could think of bringin' something along myself." He made a wide, encompassing gesture.

"Oh, don't," said Lucinda, remembering the smells. "We'll bring plenty for all—Tony and I." She was already reckoning that six of everything would make arithmetic easy.

They came home round-about-ways. It was past four when Lucinda climbed the stairs to the Misses Peters' parlor and found Uncle Earle, his big length stretched out in a chair. He was reading *The Peterkin Papers* and he gave a prodigious wink and said: "This must be Snoodie. I'm glad she's come home."

Lucinda giggled, threw herself upon him; her lips found the small patch between chop-whiskers pleasant for kissing. "You've come to have supper with me," she suggested hopefully.

"Better than that."

"You've come to take me home with you. More Mr. Shakespeare."

"I'm afraid it might be more Aunt Emily. Better wait a week and—what is it you children say when you're swinging, and let yourself go?"

"Oh—let the old cat die."

"Exactly! We'd better do that." Again he winked. Lucinda giggled. "Have a third guess, Snoodie."

The best she could do was to guess that they were going somewhere, but where and why—that was beyond her. Uncle Earle put *The Peterkin Papers* back on the shelf, commenting: "How does it happen I've never read that before? I've heard about it but never came across a copy." He was drawing Lucinda down upon his knees, his big, rumbling voice was checked to a quiet intimacy. "You see, Snoodie, your Aunt Emily has brought the gazelles up to read *Elsie Dinsmore*. What else they read, barring *Pilgrim's Progress* and the *Bible*, doesn't seem to matter. Shocking state of affairs, but long ago I gave it up. It doesn't do to have more than one person interfering in a family. A fine woman, your Aunt Emily, if you know how to take her."

Lucinda judged that Uncle Earle did; for her part, she preferred to take somebody else—anybody. The rumbling voice went on: "The case stands thus: by another week I'll have your Aunt Emily where she'll be willing to make a bargain. You to mind your manners and put a halter on that tongue of yours; she to allow you to have supper with the gazelles. But sewing time we'll arrange to spend in the library together with Mr. Shakespeare. How's that?"

"Elegant! Uncle Earle, I don't see how you can be so nice, married to Aunt Emily. If you belonged to me just as a friend —not as Aunt Emily's second husband— —"

Uncle Earle shut Lucinda up. "I said—a halter on your tongue. I should have said a double hitching around your jaw." He kissed her very tenderly. "Tut-tut, you'll outgrow it. You've got to. Think of the young men who'll want to fall in love with you and can't, because of that tongue!"

He got up, sprawling Lucinda to the floor. He beat his hands together and wagged his head in a sort of pantomime of warning. Then he thrust his hand into a pocket, drew out two yellow slips of cardboard and shook them in Lucinda's face. "How about going to the theatre tonight? Think the school teacher will let you? And we'll dine well—wherever you choose."

Lucinda went to hunt up Miss Peters. She and Miss Nettie were in the work-room. Having admitted Aunt Emily's husband she had thought it better to leave him alone, having no way of knowing what kind of person he might be. Lucinda cleared up all doubt, however: "You ought to be in, talking to him. He's about the most interesting man you'd chance on. And I'm home safe. Nothing ate us up or magicked us off. Now I'm invited out for a regular ranzy-tanzy." Lucinda clasped her hands together in eager petition, "Oh, Miss Peters, come in and tell Uncle Earle I can go!" Lucinda caught at her dress and dragged her behind skipping feet into the parlor.

Five minutes and Lucinda was in the run-way; putting on her best bib and tucker, a plum-colored plaid silk with a China silk guimpe and plum-colored velvet to trim it. In it she felt very splendid. Hand in hand she and Uncle Earle stood on a corner of Broadway to see if Mr. Gilligan might not come along without a fare; and he did. It started the evening off right. Lucinda did the introducing generously; the man driving the hansom cab and the man about to be driven felt themselves and the whole world kin. The hole in the roof of the cab was kept open and pleasant conversation passed up and down.

Lucinda chose Louis Sherry's for dinner. "It's nice to dine with your friends," she explained to Uncle Earle, "especially when they help you out of trouble," and she told the story of Tony's fruit-stand, of Patrolman M'Gonegal's bribing and of how Jerry Hanlon cleaned up the bad boys on Eighth Avenue. "Now Tony Coppino's one of my best friends. Uncle Earle, you'd like him."

"Not a doubt of it," Uncle Earle laid down his knife and fork and considered Lucinda seriously. "Snoodie, do you know that the scientists think they've discovered something very wonderful—something they call an antitoxin for diphtheria. They punch it into you, and instead of your getting all choked up and dying with the disease you get well. A remarkable discovery, if it works."

He picked up his knife and fork and went on with his roast guinea-hen. Lucinda wondered what diphtheria had to do with Tony Coppino. But Uncle Earle had a way of stopping and then going on again, like a balky horse. So she waited. A moment and the knife and fork were down: "You're getting a sort of vaccination this year. If you don't know it now, you'll find it out some day. But it's going to keep you from dying of a terrible disease."

Lucinda was filled with amazement. She put down her knife and fork, even though she was eating guinea-hen for the first time in her life and liked it tremendously. "What is the disease?" she asked solemnly.

"Snobbishness—priggishness—the Social Register. I don't

care a damn what you call it, Snoodie, as long as you get your antitoxin before the disease gets you."

Lucinda began to laugh. She choked on the guinea-hen until Louis Sherry, himself, came up and thumped her on the back and started it down the right way. She knew on the spot what Uncle Earle meant, or at least she sensed it. Still red in the face and her eyes feeling poppy she gave him an impish grin: "I'll bet you I never get in the Social Register. I'll be the one honest-to-God member of the family that stays out. What do you bet?"

"Five thousand dollars," said Uncle Earle, laughing. And he paid that debt by way of a codicil in his will when Lucinda had doubled her age of ten and forgotten all about it.

The play they saw was called *The Merry Monarch*, a musical play. In it Lucinda made the acquaintance of an actor called Francis Wilson who made them merry along with himself; who made them laugh until their ribs ached and the curtain came down to give them blessed relief. Uncle Earle said once between curtains: "There's genius for you, in the great art of merry-making. We give too little importance to it. Why there are times I'd exchange a hundred dollars for one good laugh."

A hundred dollars, thought Lucinda; a great deal of money. She laughed at the very notion of it and leaned over the arm of the seat between them. I'll bring you a laugh next Saturday for nothing. Cross my heart."

Driving home that night in somebody else's hansom cab Lucinda drowsed against Uncle Earle's shoulder. How was it that she belonged so comfortably to him? The gazelles belonged entirely to Aunt Emily, and there were times when she didn't feel that she belonged to her own parents. But with Uncle Earle it was different. Tables and chairs, city blocks, an ocean might be between them, and yet she would always feel close to him as she felt now. Something more besides words and looks and laughter passed between them and held them together. She hoped she would go through year after year, knowing that she could put out her hand—like this —and feel his big one closing over it. To buckle on roller skates and go sweeping through the city alone was splendid; but it was splendid in another way to grow sleepy against Uncle Earle's shoulder to the jog-jog-jog of the cab, and feel that I'll-always-look-after-you-Snoodie in the pressure of his big hand.

The next day, Sunday, at half-past four there came a knock at the parlor door. There stood Mr. Gilligan in his high leather boots, his top hat, the buttons on his coat shining like scoured tin plates. "'Tis tea for three and griddle bread," he said, grinning. "Will ye be after comin' for it?"

Joyfully went Lucinda, taking the guitar with her. "It's awfully nice of you and Mrs. Gilligan to invite me," she explained, "so I thought you might like some music."

"Ye play that fiddle-thing we fetched over?" Mr. Gilligan asked it proudly.

"I think I must have been born playing it. I can't remember a time when I didn't. Johanna says I was found under a cabbage; mama says the stork brought me. Either way, it doesn't matter, but I do like to think I was playing the fandango when I arrived."

They found Mrs. Gilligan greasing the griddle and washing the currants. Lucinda went into the kitchen to help and explained to Mrs. Gilligan that she was glad they didn't have a dining-room; she never yet had eaten griddle bread outside a kitchen, and she never could. Mrs. Gilligan was round as a dumpling, red as an apple; her hair was combed upwards and ended in a doughnut on the top of her head. She called Lucinda "wee lamb," and Lucinda got jumbled in her thinking, trying to decide whether Mrs. Gilligan looked like Johanna grown old, or Johanna looked like Mrs. Gilligan grown young.

The kitchen was snug and the right size for three. There were candles on the table, and a red geranium, grown from slips. There were ham and Irish potatoes, gooseberry jam, and the griddle bread. Lucinda hung over the stove as it cooked and watched the currants come to the top and pop through. Cut pie-ways, she and Mr. Gilligan ran a race with the butter to see who could spread on the most. After it was eaten down to the last slice, and not a crumb left for Miss Manners, Lucinda took the guitar out of its case and sang those Irish songs she had had from Johanna.

She sat on the kitchen table so the Gilligans could hear without peeling an ear while they washed up. She sang "The Young May Moon," "The Cruiskeen Lawn," "Kitty of Coleraine." She found Mr. Gilligan had a lip for music and together they finished up with the "Kerry Dancers" and the "Wearin' o' the Green."

Seven o'clock came too soon. "Faith, ye no sooner come in than ye go out. What kind of a visit is that, tell me?" demanded Mrs. Gilligan.

"I'll come again," promised Lucinda.

"I'll be seein' that Gilligan fetches ye soon, wee lamb."

Outside the cab Mr. Gilligan clucked and snapped his whip and asked every turn of a block, "Are ye ridin' easy?"

Inside, Lucinda was wrapt in a thick quietude. For once she had no wish to talk. Years later she was to read a pilgrim's song of Tolstoi's, but all that the great Russian writer put into words was sung by Lucinda in silence that night. She, too, would have blessed this fair world, the sky above her, the road going home, strangers and brothers. She, too, would have caught all these in a great rapture to her heart.

When Mr. Gilligan swung her to the pavement in front of Miss Lucy, honey's, brownstone front she shouted with the boatswain of *The Tempest*: "Cheerily our heart!" And when Mr. Gilligan saw her to her door and wished her "fair sleep with happy dreams" she laid her cheek to the panel and repeated solemnly: "We are such stuff as dreams are made on; and our little life is rounded with a sleep." She cupped her hand as if life lay there in it, rounded, perfect; then she flattened her hand to pat the silver buttons on Mr. Gilligan's coat. "Thank you, Mr. Gilligan, I've had an elegant time. Gra-ma-chree ma cruiskeen, Shlanthe gal mavourneen, Gra-ma-chree a cooleen bawn, bawn, bawn, O! Gra-ma-chree a cooleen bawn!" She sang Mr. Gilligan down the stairs and out through the front door.

October 12th, 189—

Tony and I have had an adventure. Glory be to God—if it hadn't been for my nose, I might turn into an old Rags-an'-Bottles myself. Wouldn't mama be surprized!

All Saturday night I dreamed about a mountain of rags. I was climbing it, or trying to, for way at the top was a huge breast-pin with precious stones. It was as big as our soup toureen. But every time I climbed a little way I slipped back more. I never did get to the top.

I guess finding treasures in rubbish is like having jam at the Queen of Hearts'—jam tomorrow and jam yesterday, but never jam today.

Now if Aunt Emily had come round to see me I'd have known it was just to keep an eye on my respectability. But Uncle Earle came because he wanted to. And what do you think! After ten long years I have a nick-name at last—just like Trinket. Uncle Earle calls me Snoodie—from the Peterkin Papers. It would be Uncle Earle who thought of it.

October 18th.

Another Saturday. Another picnic. Old Rags came just as he promised. Miss Peters was awfully curious about the extra sandwiches; but I explained Tony and I didn't have enough last time. Which is true. I didn't trouble to explain about old Rags. I don't like to worry people—especially anyone nice like Miss Peters.

Old Rags brought me a present—a brooch. He said he found

it in a purple dress last week. It's magnificent. Gold with jewels. At least that's what old Rags said when he presented it, he said Here young lady is something handsome, diamonds and emerald I should say. And diamonds and emeralds it's going to be until I die. The brooch is locked up in my desk. I shall show it to nobody. And what do you think! We rode all the way down to Fifty-Ninth Street with old Rags! We sat on the seat in the cart, the bells jangling over us; and half the way I held the reins and said giddap to Minnie, and the other half Tony did. The best part of it was pretending that Aunt Emily might drive past in her Victoria and see me. Wouldn't that have been a pretty kettle of fish! I'm still not sure what she would have done about it. But I was seen. My godmother—Aunt Ellen Douglas drove by and when she saw me she raised those glasses on a hook that she has and stared straight at me. But I guess it was too much for her to believe. Someday I'll tell Aunt Ellen—she'd only laugh. I've made up music to go with Ariel's songs. It sounds awfully pretty. I make it up a little different every time, but when it gets where it stays the same, I'm going to sing it to Uncle Earle. Won't he be surprized to find a composer in the family!

CHAPTER V

THANKSGIVING

IN that year of the nineties when Lucinda was skating up and down New York, Thanksgiving was more of a day. You set it aside, with anticipation; you recovered from it with fortitude. And you made it a point to be thankful openly and with devotion.

Lucinda avoided the devotion, but she wrote in her diary everything that she could be thankful for, and there was much. First on the list came the number of Thanksgiving dinners. Everybody Lucinda had ever known, it seemed, woke up just before that last Thursday in November and remembered her orphanage.

Miss Lucy, honey, from downstairs invited her to partake of wild turkey, from Virginia. Mr. Gilligan stopped between fares to say that Mrs. Gilligan would be proud to have her. Johanna wrote from across the river in Jersey, where she was living with a married sister until Lucinda's parents returned. Would she come and eat goose with them? Johanna had been thinking long for her these many weeks. Michael would come early to fetch her, whoever Michael might be. Aunt Emily wrote in no uncertain terms that she would be expected there, without skates and with good manners. Her godmother, Aunt Ellen Douglas McCord, without children but with a great regard for them, sent her maid Annie over with a note:

I am ashamed to have neglected you. But it is a form of flattery. I know how well you can take care of yourself. However, come to Thanksgiving dinner. It will be late, seven o'clock. But you are a strong and sensible child; you will fit in with your elders and digest the dinner. Your Uncle Tom McCord especially wants to see you, and Shoestrings has missed his romps with you. Afterwards we go to the Robert Ingersolls' for a play.

Mr. Collyer, who had christened her, stopped her after church to say they would be delighted to take her home after the Thanksgiving service; Mr. Spindler of the Gedney House sent Buttons up to say that he and Mrs. S. hoped for the pleasure of her company at two o'clock. Lucinda told Miss Nettie that she was positive no one else in the city had so many invitations: "Isn't it terrible to have all these turkeys gobbling at me—just asking me to eat them! And here's one goose; I mustn't forget Johanna's goose."

She put into action that New England thrift she had inherited from Grandmother Wyman. She arranged with Miss Lucy, honey, to invite the Browdowskis in her place. She said nothing about the possibility of their being too poor to have a good Thanksgiving dinner. She pointed out their loneliness, their lack of friends. "Of course, it means places for three instead of one; but I do eat an awful lot, Miss Lucy. Do ask them. I don't think they'd eat much more." She wrote Johanna and asked if she couldn't come on Saturday afternoon, and help pick the goose bare. She skated down to the Gedney House and coaxed Mrs. Spindler to let her come the day after Thanksgiving and eat turkey leavings. "I always think warmed-over turkey is better than fresh, don't you, honestly, Mrs. Spindler?"

She accepted without reservation her godmother's invitation; it was the only one she could accept and have Aunt Emily forgive her the sin of not spending Thanksgiving with her and the docile daughters. For Aunt Ellen Douglas McCord was a more important person in every way than Aunt Emily; and Lucinda had grown wise enough in her ten years to know the value of impressing Aunt Emily. Also she adored Shoestrings, the Welsh terrier.

When the day came she put on the plum-colored silk plaid. She teased Miss Peters long and hard to be allowed to go on skates. "I'm so skatey today, just chuck full of excitement. And Shoestrings will love to be taken out on skates. He's never been. Please, Miss Peters!"

"You have on your best white stockings and your best

dress. If you fall down, I don't know what might happen."

Lucinda was in her positive mood. "I won't. I never fall down—that is, when I really take pains not to. Please, Miss Peters, hoofing is so pokey."

"Oh, let her," said Miss Nettie, and that settled it.

Away went Lucinda in her best form, skimming pavements, dashing over curbs and across streets. She was particularly exuberant because she had taken Miss Nettie's shears that morning, unbeknownst, and cut off the legs of her underdrawers. She had kept her promise to her mother and put on the plaguey old things the last week in October. For almost a month now she had put them on every morning, loathing them, wrapping the end of the legs around her ankles and patiently trying to pull her stockings neatly over them.

But could she? Never! It always ended by the drawers riding triumphantly up her legs with the stockings. She would try once—twice—a half-dozen times with patience. Then temper would get her. She would jerk; she would say those things forbidden a young Wyman; such as Darn it, and Hell, and Jumping Jehoshaphat! And at last she would leave them, pulled half up her legs, making her look bandy-legged and feeling as ugly as Satan, choked in sin. The underdrawers were working against the roller skates, putting her on the verge of tantrums. No knowing when they would break out again, like measles.

Then had come the idea. She could keep her promise to mama and avoid the tantrums in one fell swoop. Early Thanksgiving morning she had crept into the work-room, taken Miss Nettie's shears and cut her drawers all round about. She felt sinful and virtuous in the same breath, and it made her think of the nursery rhyme which she sang exultantly as she cut:

> "There was an old woman as I have heard tell.
>   She went to market her eggs for to sell;
>   She went to market all on a market day,
>   And she fell asleep on the king's highway.
>
>   Along came a peddler by the name of Stout.
>   He cut her petticoats all round about;
>   He cut her petticoats up to her knees,
>   And the old woman began for to freeze."

Now with underdrawers cut to her knees, she felt free again—herself. She had reached the tag-end of the last block skating to Aunt Ellen Douglas McCord's, her speed increasing, her head down for a final spurt. But luck interfered in the person of a slowly moving, preoccupied, fat man between Lucinda and Aunt Ellen's stoop. There was a collision. The fat man went down, his hat flew off; but Lucinda fared worse. She had worn her best gloves; every finger was now thrust out of its sheaf in public nakedness. Except for a good dusting her dress and coat had escaped; but her stockings were ruined; her knees skinned. And down each leg ran blood, plenty of blood.

"A perfect wreck," was her comment as she climbed the stoop to her godmother's door.

"You deserve it," shouted the fat man after her.

"I know it, but that doesn't make it any better." Tubbins,

the butler, opened the door, sort of hiccoughed at her, and passed her over to Annie. Annie delivered her to her god-mother in no uncertain terms. "Here's Lucinda, Mrs. Mc-Cord. We'd best be ringing for an ambulance."

But Aunt Ellen was a woman of resources. And she was Scotch. In a teagown of blue and old rose, with fur around it, she looked Lucinda over. "You've done it very thorough-ly, my dear, as you did whooping-cough and scarlet fever. Annie, get a basin of hot water, lint, and iodine."

Sponged off, bandaged; the stockings still presented a hopeless appearance. "I tell you what we'll do," said Lucin-da. She was recovering her spirits. "French children, now. Mam'selle said they wore socks all through the winter. Couldn't we make these into socks and make believe I've just come over from Paris."

The stockings were washed, dried, and socks were evolved. Lucinda came to Thanksgiving dinner bandaged, with bare legs almost to her boot-tops. They were a large party. Some Lucinda knew, some she didn't. She knew the MacDowells but she didn't care much about young Edward. He didn't care much about her, so it was mutual. But she did love Mother MacDowell and Tossie—as everyone called Ed-ward's father. The dinner was a sumptuous affair. It began with a vile mess called terrapin. Then came fish to fiddle with. By the time that Uncle Tom was carving the turkey Lucinda thought everyone ought to be too full to enjoy it. For her part she had kept empty, deliberately empty for tur-key and dessert. Only once through the dinner did Lucinda speak. That was when the wine was served out of round-bottomed bottles in straw baskets. "Once, when I was at the

Coppinos' to see their bambino they had a bottle just like
that on their kitchen table. The Coppinos are my friends—
they keep a fruit-stand."

She was sitting next to young Edward and for the first time
he appeared to take an interest in her. "Do you make friends
of people who keep fruit-stands?"

Lucinda nodded enthusiastically. "I have more than that
for friends." She checked them on the fingers of her small,
square hand: "Mr. Gilligan who drives a hansom cab, Patrolman M'Gonegal in Bryant Park, old Rags-an'-Bottles
who— —" But Aunt Ellen hushed her. "Edward, keep that
child still and listen to me. I think I can get Andrew Carnegie
interested. He says he likes music but I don't know. He can
be a terrible liar. Anyway, he ought to be as interested in
building up American music as American libraries. . . .
You could dedicate a concerto to him. . . ."

Lucinda went to sleep, her head lolling over until it came inevitably to rest on young Edward's shoulder. In the years to follow she was to wonder much about that Andrew Carnegie and what he might or might not have done for young Edward. She could hear the snapping of Aunt Ellen's fingers down those years and the look on her face when she spoke of him as that terrible Scotchman.

By nine o'clock Lucinda was wide awake again, and away they went to Mr. Ingersoll's house—to the top floor of it where there was a theatre, bigger than Lucinda's own and smaller than a real one. Half of Mr. Ingersoll's family were the actors, and half were borrowed from the neighborhood. And they gave a very good play indeed called the White Mare, or the Gray Mare or some kind of a horse. A man by the name of Anton Seidl came with three or four musicians to play for them. It was very good music; Lucinda wished she could make her guitar sound that way. She had known Robert Ingersoll since she was a baby; in her mind she matched him beside Uncle Earle and found him almost as kind and interesting. But he filled her with a terrible curiosity. Aunt Emily had said once that he didn't believe in God. He was the only person Lucinda knew who didn't. She wondered a great deal why, and never found out.

She sat up later than she had ever sat up in her life. She drove home with Aunt Ellen in her brougham and never remembered it. Uncle Tom carried her up the two flights and gave her to Miss Nettie to put to bed. All Lucinda knew was that she woke up the next morning in the folding bed and remarked to herself: "That's funny. I wonder was it the gray mare who brought me!"

Having no school that day Lucinda borrowed Trinket for the morning. Trinket had found her tongue since Lucinda had begun borrowing her. She had everything to tell about the Thanksgiving dinner they had had with Miss Lucy. Trinket had gotten the wishbone; she had had two dishes of ice cream. Afterwards her father had brought down his violin; Lady Ross had played the piano, and together they had made music for all the guests in the two houses. Later, Lucinda was to hear more about it from Mr. Night Owl.

"Your friend Mr. Browdowski—Mr. Serge Browdowski—is some fiddler. Mark my word—when you grow up you'll speak with bated breath when you mention his name."

"So he's good?" asked Lucinda.

"He's one of the best."

"Then why is he so poor?"

"Most great men are poor when they're young. Poverty and genius hook fingers. You'll find that out some day. Probably your friend upstairs is playing every night in some cheap café or theatre when he ought to be a concert violinist."

Lucinda and Mr. Night Owl made a compact. They would talk about Trinket's father to everybody they knew—high and low. Then some day something truly might happen and the world would discover Mr. Serge Browdowski.

Lucinda skated down to the Gedney House and had turkey leavings and a very pleasant time with the Spindlers. After dinner Mrs. S. always took a nap; and Mr. S. was doubtful about having Lucinda on his mind for the rest of the afternoon. "I guess you'd like me to go." Lucinda still believed that honesty was the best policy. Moreover she had pleasant things on her own mind. She could answer bells with But-

tons, racing down the red plush carpeted halls and seeing who could make the biggest spark on the doorknobs at the end; or she could call on Mrs. Caldwell and Pygmalion, or—
— She had come face to face with a better idea.

"You know, Mr. Spindler, I'd like to know those new people you have in your house. I mean the little girl about my age; her grandmother and grandfather are actors."

The manager laughed. "All right, come along. She's a pretty lonely little girl. I guess she would like to know you."

Together they went up to the top floor back. Mr. Spindler knocked and a little girl, just Lucinda's size, with flaxen pigtails and a little snub nose opened the door. The next thing Lucinda knew she was inside, the door was closed, and Aleda Solomon and she were looking each other well over.

"Do you play dolls?" asked Lucinda finally.

"No!" said Aleda. "Do you?"

"No. What do you play?"

"Mostly theatre."

"Elegant. So do I. Only I guess I don't play it the way you do."

Aleda walked to the great wardrobe against the wall, and to the two enormous trunks that banked it on either side. She threw open the doors of the wardrobe; she flung back the lids of the trunks. If she had been Aladdin's uncle showing the treasure of the cave to Aladdin the effect could not have held more enchantment. There were the soft deep glow of velvets, the shimmer of satins and brocades, the glitter of gold thread and lace. There were crowns and chaplets, jeweled, and rings and bracelets and earrings. There were wigs and sandals; hats and scarfs and long colored plumes.

"Golly!" said Lucinda. "Are they yours?"

"They belong to my grandmother. When she was young she was a great Shakespearean actress. Now she plays old parts, but she plays them well. And don't think that because she is old she is not still beautiful."

"Oh, I don't," Lucinda was willing to believe anything, with the splendor of wardrobe and trunks before her eyes.

They stood shifting on young feet, still uncertain of each other; until Aleda said impatiently. "Well, what do you want to be?"

"What do you mean—what do I want to be?"

"Well—there are the costumes. You can be the Queen in Hamlet or Ophelia or Juliet! Or you can be just a queen or a princess. See?"

Lucinda wanted to be just a queen. But she knew that a jeweled crown would look out of joint on a croppy-boy's head like hers. She said so, honestly; and out of one of the trunks Aleda produced a flaxen wig, with long braids. "You can be a queen with that on. Try it. I'll show you."

On went the wig with Aleda's help. The braids nearly swept the floor. Lucinda thought she looked ravishing. She chose a blue velvet robe, a dazzling crown. By this time, something was happening to the inside of her. She had entered a new world, as real as any she had discovered in her ten years, and she trod it with ecstasy.

Lucinda strutted while Aleda chose her costume. Then the play began in earnest. They told each other who they were, in what castle they lived, what great events were about to happen, and they discoursed together accordingly. They thou-ed and thy-ed and said Yes, my Lord, and No, my Lady.

"You are the queen—a Scottish queen. I am your lady-in-waiting. There is a plot to unthrow the king," said Aleda.

"Where will he be unthrown to?"

"Outside the kingdom. Probably Russia."

"Russia is a long way off," objected Lucinda. "The Atlantic Ocean would be nearer."

"Then he'd be drowned."

"Well, that wouldn't matter. He isn't in the play anyway."

"He's your husband. You wouldn't want him to drown, would you?" Aleda disapproved of Lucinda's lack of emotion.

"I never had a husband. I might not care a snap." Lucinda illustrated and caught the look on Aleda's face. "Of course, if you want me to mind—why—I'll jump in and save him."

"Not in those clothes!"

"Let's begin again."

The lady-in-waiting was to overhear the plot in the queen's garden and tell the queen. The queen would save the king and reward the lady-in-waiting. A button bag did splendidly for a purse of gold. The floor was strewn with artificial flowers to make a garden, and Lucinda ended up with Ariel's song supposedly sung to the king:

> "While you here do snoring lie,
>   Open-eyed conspiracy
>   His time doth take.
>   If of life you keep a care,
>   Shake off slumber and beware;
>   Awake, Awake!"

Aleda's grandparents arrived just as the song came to a

dramatic close. They were young for grandparents; Mr. Solomon, short, nervous, and very spanky looking; Mrs. Solomon, small, tight in her dresses, stepping high and looking pleased. Lucinda thought she had the kind of a face that could be said to be sad and sweet. She embraced Aleda; she embraced Lucinda. She expressed excessive joy at Aleda's finding a playmate. "Your people don't belong to the theatre by any chance?" she asked Lucinda.

"Not exactly belong, but go," Lucinda tried to make it sound almost the same thing. She had never had a girl playmate like Aleda before. She wanted terribly to be invited to come again. She undressed slowly down to her own pinafore hoping the wish would spread and be caught by the Solomons. And sure enough—before the crown and wig were laid away Mrs. Solomon said: "Come again—come whenever you like. It gets to be terribly lonely for Aleda when we're rehearsing a new play and doing an old one. Like to go some Wednesday matinée?"

Would she! Lucinda was too full of rapturous excitement to ring for the elevator and ride down. She needed to scoot, and scoot hard. It would take her five flights and an extra hall or two to bring her to the hotel lobby and slow her down to reach the door with good deportment. Such luck! Exciting things just never happened to you when you were piloted around by Johanna or Mam'selle.

Dang it all, as old Rags-an'-Bottles would say, who wanted to stand still and let the clock do all the moving? Who wanted to walk through lonely years, right foot, left foot, and never change step—never skip, run, or skate? She thought of Gonzalo's speech to the men from Naples. Like them she was of brave mettle; she could lift the moon out of her sphere—if it should continue in it five weeks without changing.

She came to the second floor—her feet stubbing hard into the nap of the red plush carpet, her skates dangling over her back. And then the elevator opened to expel a guest and there before her stood no less a one than the lady who might be the heathen Chinee Buttons had told about. Face to face they stood, and Lucinda let out a staccato sign of rapture. The lady smiled, Lucinda smiled. She did more than that; her tongue took its habitual freedom and raced squarely into the encounter.

"Goody," said Lucinda, "I did want to see you. Buttons says you're simply elegant, but I didn't like to ask Mr. Spindler to introduce me. But now we've met you don't mind, do you?"

The small, finely molded Asiatic lady shook her head. "You speak very quick, my dear. What is it you want? I do not know your English."

What did Lucinda want? Now that she was faced squarely with it, she did not know herself. Her roving eye took in the magnificence of all this lady wore: furs, worth a king's ransom—jewels, worth more. And she was beautiful in a wholly strange way. The Queen of Sheba might have looked like her, on her way to Solomon, or Cleopatra in Anthony's barge. Could she, Lucinda Wyman, a ten-year-old roller-skater of this great city expect to have friendly traffic with such an enchanted one? She must explain—explaining was also a habit. "I thought," she said it with hesitation, "you would be so very interesting to know. I do like interesting people. But of course, you wouldn't have time for anybody like me."

"Time? You mean I do not have hours empty with nothing to put into them! *Mon Dieu*, I have a day full of time with nothings to do. And I like little children very much. Come. I think I have something pretty to show you."

She led the way to a corner suite. Lucinda marked its number—207. She opened the door and the splendor of what was inside came out and struck Lucinda flat, as she told Tony afterwards. Never had she seen anything like it. The parlor walls were hung with rugs; there were splendid lamps hanging from doorways, side brackets, and the ceiling. These were of brass set with colored glass, and they made dancing spots of colored light upon the woodwork and window shades. Taking up a quarter of the room and projecting out from the corner was something oriental but wholly unknown to Lucinda. It was a broad, cushioned platform, hung with heavy curtains of brown and rust and green, studded with tiny pieces of looking glass. Cushions of every size and pattern, some woven with gold, some soft leather were heaped on the platform. On the walls back of the platform hung weapons, curious long curved swords, thin daggers, broad-bladed hacking knives; and there was one dagger with a jeweled hilt, hanging in its scabbard. Among the cushions were dolls dressed in oriental costumes. Lucinda stood and gaped; her eyes picked at once a Japanese doll and called him Nanky Pu. Years afterwards she was to know tawdry imitations of this very thing—and hear them called cozy-corners.

The lady clapped her hands, for all the world like someone in the Arabian Nights. Out of a small alcove came a dark maid-servant. "Take my wraps. Bring sweetmeats." She drew Lucinda down with her upon the platform. "Look, is she not nice? This is a little Turkish girl, and this one is my little boy from Japan. You like?"

"I love them," said Lucinda, spreading her meagre lap to hold them all. The maid-servant brought a tray upon which were many little brass dishes, each holding a different sweetmeat or nut. "I am inside a book of fairy-tales," laughed Lucinda. "You are a princess. Your name is Zayda—or—or——" She racked her brains for more names from Washington Irving's *Legends of the Alhambra*.

"I am no one but Mrs. Isaac Grose. I am so sorry. But you can give me a name you like. What shall it be? Or you will call me just your princess, and I will call you my friend—my friendling."

Together they ate Turkish paste, sugared almonds, salted pistachio nuts and candied fruit. The princess brought out a lacquered box, and out of this some cigarettes. She lighted one, lay back on the cushions, and smoked. Lucinda had never seen, had never dreamed it even possible that a woman could smoke. It only made the whole ending of that day appear more unbelievable. Together they laughed about nothing at all because it was good to laugh; and the princess told of adventures in eastern lands; she might have been Scheherezade telling one of the Thousand and One Nights tales.

And then the adventure was shattered like a goblet. The door was swung open with a crash. Inside, on the threshold, stood a squat, swarthy man. He had eyes, black and deep like pools of tar; he had a black beard, cut square, and the blue glass from the hanging lantern played upon it making it a luminous blue beard. His eyes were prepared to be angry, Lucinda thought; and then they changed like the eyes of a sorcerer. What he said was: "It is a child. That is good. I heard laughter and words and I thought . . ." He stopped, came forward and rubbed a dark, hairy hand on the cheek of the princess. "Never mind what I thought, Elise. Tell me who the little friend is."

Lucinda spared no effort in getting her things on and getting out of the door. The man with the blue beard had given her the horrors; and the more he stood, looking and questioning her, the greater the horrors grew. She was like a silly baby, stammering, "I must go. Truly, I must go." And go she did, dashing away with her skates clanking; rushing for the stairs, hearing the voice of the princess following her down, as if in a dream. It called: "Come back, my friendling! Very much I need you for the empty hours."

Not until she reached the street did she realize how late she was. The lamps were all lighted; everyone was hurrying home. She must hurry and explain why she had forgotten time and everything. Miss Peters and Miss Nettie were in the parlor; it was after six o'clock and they were frightened. She marched in bravely enough. She said: "I know. It's dreadful. I am awfully sorry. You must punish me, Miss Peters. Mama would; she would punish me very severely. I deserve it." But she never told of the princess or the man with the blue beard. She knew if she did that she would be forbidden to go back and she knew that she must go. Anyone who has had the door of fairyland opened to them will understand how inevitably one must go back—again and again and again.

November 23rd, 189—

Life has been higgledy-piggledy. I love it that way. Almost a hundred invitations to Thanksgiving. I ate Turkey with Aunt Ellen on Thursday, leavings with the Spindlers on Friday, goose with Johanna on Saturday—Michael is the sister's husband, and Sunday—after church I spent with Uncle Earle. We read a Midsummer Night's Dream and I like Bottom and Puck best. I think I am putting a girdle 'round New York—only it takes me longer to do it than it took Puck to put it round the world. I have two new friends. Aleda and the Princess Zayda. That isn't her name but I play it is. I've told the Miss Peterses all about Aleda, and I'm going to have her here for supper next week. But the Princess is my very own secret, locked up.

Nov. 27th.

I've spent all my money on things for The Tempest. I had to go to church without a nickel to put in the place. While I was talking in the vestibule with the Sexton in came Mr. Gideon—he passes the plate down our side of the aisle. I thought it would be terribly embarrassing to have him pass the plate to me and not have my regular nickel so I explained and he was awfully nice. He said Lucinda I'll leave you out of the collection until Christmas is over and no one need be the wiser. I call that being a gentleman.

What I'd like to know is who gets the collection. It's a lot of money—nickels, dimes, quarters and bills. Where does it go?

CHAPTER VI

BORN IS THE KING OF ISRAEL

LUCINDA had the gift for festival. She spread out Christmas to last from Saint Nicholas Eve until Twelfth Night; and burned the greens on the hearth with a choked feeling of utter desolation. She had confided to Mr. Night Owl that she liked the Dutch side of New York. So on December 6 Lucinda skated in pace with his long strides, and together they visited the landmarks of New Amsterdam. Mr. Night Owl had a weakness for the old Knickerbockers. It was like playing the wildest game of Blind Man's Buff to close your eyes, give a hand to him, and let him steer

you down Tenth Avenue to old Chelsea, calling: "Gang-
way," or "Low bridge," or "Up curb!" until you opened your
eyes again and saw the very house where Clement Moore
had written his "Visit from Saint Nicholas." And then to
close your eyes again and go down what used to be called
Love Lane, to that very place where once upon a time the
Dutch had built a stockade clear across the island to keep the
Britishers out.

Tuckered out, that's what she was when she came home
and found Miss Nettie had invited Trinket down for supper
and together they had set the cutting table with the dolls'
teaset; a surprise for Lucinda. Luck had given Miss Nettie
two children to love that winter. Her ears as well as Lucinda's
were cocked to hear Trinket's laughter. It was bubbling over
now, and Trinket's tiny feet had learned their way to dancing.

Trinket would drink dozens of cups of milk—doll's size,
while she had to be coaxed with an ordinary mugful; she
would eat numberless bread and butter tartines off a doll's
plate, and spoon her egg out of a tiny egg-cup. This was play
to Trinket, and she had never begun to play until that first
day Lucinda had borrowed her.

The nights Trinket came to supper, and the number of
them grew each week, she and Lucinda would play house
afterwards, washing the tiny dishes, putting them away, making believe this and that; every time there was something
new to make believe. Lucinda read aloud *The Tempest* and
Trinket listened as captivated as if she were listening to
Mother Goose. But the best part was always the last, when
Lucinda would take the big rocker, and Trinket would climb
into her lap for Lucinda's singing. There was the *Saint*

Nicholas Song Book to sing from. Out of it came a song about a shark, another about a mermaid. There was the Valentine song that began: "O loveliest little lady mine! What shall I bring for your Valentine?" and the rollicking song of the Big Brown Farmer who hoed and the Little Brown Bee who hummed.

From *Water Babies* came: "I once had a dear little doll, dears," and Trinket thought Lucinda was singing about her own little doll in the red dress and white kid slippers. No matter what was sung first and middle, Lucinda always sang last, "Froggie would a-wooing go," for that was Trinket's favorite.

As Christmas neared Trinket's cheeks began to glow red like hollyberries; and when Mr. Browdowski would come to carry her off to bed he would look down at the two in the big rocker and say in a deep husky voice: "What are you playing at tonight, my Lucinda? Are you the big sister to our Trinket —or the fairy godmother—or the little mother—or just the good doctor?"

It was habit for Lucinda to reach out for the world with fancy rather than with emotion. Not until she was grown was she to know that her family had always looked upon her as a cold, undemonstrative child who would stand stiff and unresisting while she was being kissed; visibly glad to have it over with; that rarely did she speak of love or proffer affection. But those who knew her that tenth year knew her as a child eager with her loving and her showing of it. She, herself, was conscious of a kind of awe at the way certain things and people stirred her from within, especially those people who gave generously of their trust to her.

Snow came; first in flurries that melted away by midday; then in a heavy, lazy falling of flakes that covered window-sills, pavements and street. The roller skates were put away reluctantly in Lucinda's wardrobe; leggings and overshoes came out of their wrappings, and Lucinda looked with longing at a bright red sled in the window of the little toy-station-ery-and-tobacco shop on Eighth Avenue. She wished she had it to take Trinket riding in the snow. She thought about it and thought about it and dreamed about it at night in the folding bed.

It cost a good deal of money, that sled. She couldn't buy it, but she could do something else for Trinket. She could have a tree for her. She talked it over first with Miss Peters and Miss Nettie. "I'll have to go to Aunt Emily's for Christmas Eve—same as usual. I guess I'll have to keep on going there as long as I live—ninety years, perhaps. The Waters girls, and the Brown girls and the gazelles and I will be white tarlaton angels, just as we've been since we could walk. And we'll sing carols and wave our star-wands and Aunt Emily will say, same as usual, 'When are you going to learn to be graceful, Lucinda?'" Lucinda ended with a giggle. "But on Christmas morning can't we have a special Christmas tree for Trinket—a little tree and make all the things for it, and have it a big surprise?"

She talked it over with Mrs. Browdowski one day when Trinket was out with her father; and discovered that Trinket had never had a tree in all the four years of her tiny life. So that made it more exciting than ever—to have for Trinket her very first tree! The more she thought about it the more posi-tive she was that they couldn't keep all the fun of it to themselves—just she and Miss Peters and Miss Nettie. Miss Lucy, honey, must come, Mr. Night Owl, Lady Ross. And of course the Gilligans and Uncle Earle; and Aleda, down from the Gedney House; Tony, and perhaps he might bring the bambino. There was no end to the people she would like to invite.

She couldn't invite people to a Christmas tree and not have a present for everybody. She had spent all her allowance up to Saint Nicholas Day on *The Tempest*. Where could she get money for presents? How—where—how—where? The silly old question ran around in her head like a kitten after a spool. If she could earn some money now!

She dropped in one afternoon to see Mrs. Caldwell and that charming old lady gave her her first idea. The snow was bad; the pavements slippery; she was afraid of falling; Pygmalion was not getting out for his walk. "If you would come every day, my dear, then I wouldn't worry. He loves to go with you better than anyone else; and that would help towards your Christmas fund. You would be earning it."

"How perfectly glorious! It doesn't seem right to earn money so pleasantly. Mama never paid me to do anything except what I positively hated to do."

"That's too bad. I think money ought to be always earned pleasantly. Think of how much gayer the world would be if everybody went to work in the morning knowing he was going to do something he enjoyed doing all day!" As Mrs. Caldwell said it Lucinda thought she looked more than ever like the pictures of Queen Victoria, with her lace cap and her chunky chin and her sleepy, kind old eyes.

Afterwards she stopped at suite 207 and found her Princess Zayda very sad; and then all of a sudden very glad when she found who had come knocking at her door. "I have fresh Turkish candy for you and a bowl of litchi nuts. You will like, yes?"

So full was Lucinda with her news of earning money for Christmas that she could talk of nothing else. Twice, three times, the princess tried to put in a word and failed utterly. Not until Lucinda had run down like a clock did she discover that an idea like Mrs. Caldwell's could be carried like scarlet fever; only with pleasanter results. "Keep without moving, little Lucinda, and I speak. My 'usband say I talk the English very bad. Every day after you take the little dog for promenade, you shall come here and teach me the English. So— you like earn more money?"

After that, every day until Christmas, Lucinda was as busy as Mr. Gilligan with his hansom cab. At three she took Pygmalion out, putting on his blanket, sometimes his overshoes. For an hour she visited with her friends up and down Broadway; sometimes Aleda came with her and they talked of plays. Aleda knew hundreds of plays, it seemed, and she would tell the stories of them. Sometimes Lucinda went on Eighth Avenue, to renew acquaintance with Jerry Hanlon and see if Tony was minding the stand. She would go into the toy-stationery-and-tobacco shop and warm her feet and Pygmalion's toes beside the stove. It was very warm and comfortable inside. Mr. and Mrs. Schultz who kept the shop always made them welcome, and Lucinda usually bought a pennyworth of coltsfoot or licorice stick so as not to wear that welcome out. Another thing she always did; it made the Schultzes laugh and gave her a great deal of satisfaction. She went around the shop and undid all the fastenings on the

jack-in-the-boxes. Out they would pop with a squeak, flap
their silly hands, and grin at Lucinda. Lucinda would always
grin back and say the same thing to each one: "There, I bet
you that feels good!"

Once Mrs. Schultz asked her: "Kindlein, why you the
boxes open like so—always?" And Lucinda answered: "Oh,
I don't know. I guess I like the squeak."

At four o'clock she was unblanketing Pygmalion in Mrs.
Caldwell's room and telling everything that had happened.
To the old lady's keen delight she made up and repeated as
actual such conversation as she and Pygmalion had had together. One day it ran this wise, and in her own heart Lucinda
had not meant it to sound more than nonsense:

"Pygmalion said, 'Lucinda let's go round on Eighth Avenue and see that elegant red sled again.'

"And I said: 'Piggy, I just can't stand to look at that sled
any more. I know I can't buy it for Trinket. Some other little
girl is going to get it eventually and it breaks my heart.'

"And Pygmalion said: 'The moral of that is—never give
up hope!' "

Pygmalion always watched her go with longing for her to
stay in his round, black, beady eyes, with loops of gold setting
them.

It took her five long breaths to scoot down the stairs and
reach suite 207. To be teaching the princess English seemed
to Lucinda the height of absurdity. "I'm only ten, after all,"
she protested once. "You should get Miss Peters. She could
teach arithmetic to a brass monkey."

"But I want you, don't you go for to see?"

"Just—*don't you see*," corrected Lucinda.

The princess had a lovely way of paying her. At five o'clock, she would take out of her lovely silver chatelaine bag two coins—one big, one small. She would hide these in her hands, hold out the hands, and Lucinda had to choose which one. Sometimes it was the little coin she got—half a dime or ten cents; sometimes it was a quarter or fifty cents. The fifty-cent days troubled Lucinda. It was too, too much for paying a little girl to tell her adored princess what not to say.

So did the Christmas fund grow apace. Lucinda arranged with Vittore to buy the tree on one of his trips to market. She got it for a quarter, very cheap. It stood for three days before Christmas in the corner of the Misses Peters' parlor and made the whole room smell like the spruce woods in Maine after a hot summer rain. It had wide-spreading branches just as she liked them; she hated a spindling tree.

Tony and Miss Nettie helped her make the decorations; Tony coming in after supper, wearing his Sunday clothes and a secret, shy smile that made him look more than ever like the young Michael Angelo. The three made cornucopias out of silver paper, pasted red decalcomanias outside, and hung them with red ribbon to the tree. Out of the scraps left over they rolled long silver icicles. They made paper chains out of tiny links of red and white and silver; and Tony cut stars out of the thin wood of the orange crates and silvered them. Lucinda coaxed Black Sarah into popping corn for clusters. The only ornaments they had to buy for the tree were the candles and tinsel. She stopped half an hour after church the Sunday before to tell Mr. Gideon how wonderful Christmas was turning out, and to thank him again for not passing the plate in her direction. "I expect that's what you'd call tact on your part. I'd like to invite you to the tree, Mr. Gideon, and that isn't tact on my part, it's real appreciation."

Mr. Gideon thanked her and said he might come and then again he might not; it would depend. But he took the Misses Peters' address down very carefully. Lucinda skated home wishing he had made up his mind then and there. If he came she'd have to have a present for him, and if he didn't she'd hate to waste it.

On the afternoon before Christmas, before it was time to go over to Aunt Emily's to be a white tarlaton angel, Lucinda and Miss Nettie made candy to fill the cornucopias. Miss Nettie's candy was almost as good as Louis Sherry's; almost. They made butter toffee and peanut crisp; and some white bonbon stuff out of confectioner's sugar and white of eggs that they rolled into balls and pressed flat between two walnut halves. They didn't crack the shells taking out the meats; and Tony glued them together and silvered them. This last touch made the tree perfectly magnificent.

"It's the nicest tree I ever had, and it will be Trinket's onliest up to now. I do hope you're as excited about it as I am, Miss Nettie." Lucinda spread sugary fingers about Miss Nettie's neck and said something that surpised them both: "I do love you, Miss Nettie."

Eleven sharp, Lucinda had said to all invited. Uncle Earle was to come secretly; all the others openly. She woke Christmas morning with a pop, for all the world like another jack coming out of its box. From the folding bed she could see the tree ready, in the corner, with all the presents on it. After the room was tidied up they would move the tree into the middle so everyone could sit around it—chairs or floor. Would she have to eat a breakfast first? She felt so full of everything else that food—pettyjohn, toast, and cocoa—seemed nonsense. She balanced around that half the tree that stood out from the corner like a sleepy penguin. There was the penwiper she had sewed for Uncle Earle. Wouldn't he boom out like an old cannon at the joke of a Christmas present sewed for him by Lucinda? There were Trinket's red mittens, and Mr. Night Owl's calendar, and everything—everything—everything done up in white paper and tied with red twine.

She had to go and pound on the Misses Peters' bedroom door and shout: "Merry Christmas! Merry Christmas!" And Miss Peters came out and was hugged and discovered to be very hard and bony under her flannelette nightgown; and Miss Nettie came out, with curlers in her hair, and was discovered to be plump and squashy under hers.

At a little before eleven, sharp, two magnificent events occurred. A messenger boy arrived and inquired for Miss Lucinda Wyman. He had a sizable box to deliver with the compliments of Mr. Simon Gideon. It was a box of Louis Sherry's very own candies. To think of Mr. Gideon being so nice! And ten minutes later up the stairs puffed Mr. Schultz from the toy-stationery-and-tobacco shop on Eighth Avenue. He puffed because he was carrying the red sled. Lucinda almost sat down with astonishment. To the sled was tied a tag and the tag read:

> *To Lucinda with a Merry Christmas,*
>   *to do with exactly as she likes.*
>   *From her friend, Pygmalion.*

"I can't wait—I can't wait—I can't wait for eleven, sharp," shouted Lucinda as they moved the tree to the middle of the room and put the red sled under the branches, right where Trinket would see it first as she came in the door. If the tree had looked beautiful upon going to bed it looked now beyond all whooping.

Uncle Earle arrived first. Lucinda was caroling by that time about the wonderful tree that all the children rejoice to see. Uncle Earle flung open the door, his arms full of packages, and Lucinda grabbed him about the middle and they danced like two clumsy bears—a big and a little one. Lucinda shouted: "I rejoice, thou rejoiceth, he, she, and it rejoices! We rejoice, you rejoice, they rejoice! Uncle Earle, I am about to split with rejoicing."

Tony came next. He brought little painted jumping-jacks that he had made to hang on the tree; one for everybody. And a sack full of oranges. "My papa says—Merry Christmas; my mama says—Merry Christmas. I say—Merry Christmas," and he thrust into Lucinda's hand a gift. It was a carved bracelet, leaves and fruit covering the circle and polished with wax to a soft finish. "My papa showed me how they carve frames for the Holy Madonna in Italy. That is how I come to make it."

"It is beautiful, Tony, perfectly beautiful! I shall wear it to every party, and keep it until I die." Lucinda made up her mind on the spot that it would be the greatest treasure she would keep secretly locked inside her desk.

When everyone had arrived and chosen chairs or floor to sit on, Lucinda counted them over to make sure none was missing: the Gilligans, Jerry Hanlon, because he wasn't mar-

ried, Miss Lucy, honey, Mr. Night Owl, Lady Ross, Aleda
Solomon and Buttons, Uncle Earle and Tony, Johanna, from
New Jersey, the Misses Peters and herself. Everyone present.
Then Uncle Earle and Tony lighted the candles while she
scooted up to the third floor and knocked three times on the
Browdowskis' door. That was the signal. Then she scooted
back again and took her place on the floor beside Tony.

And what do you think! When they came—those three
friends—Trinket was holding her mother's hand and Mr.
Browdowski—Serge Browdowski, who one day was to become very famous—came with his violin tucked under his
chin playing the French carol, "The First Noel." By the
time they had reached the wide-flung door all had joined in
the singing of it:

> "Noel—Noel—Noel—Noel—
> Born is the King of Israel."

Not a word spoken, just the singing. It was, as Lucinda
whispered to Tony, the loveliest way for Trinket to see her
first Christmas tree. She dropped her mother's hand and all
alone went around the tree touching with one finger, doll's
size, this and that. But the first thing she touched was one of
Tony's jumping-jacks. Her tiny mouth was drawn to a pucker
and out of it she blew little round "O's" like soap bubbles.

Suddenly she looked about the lighted circle and saw
many people. She hunted out Lucinda with her eyes, rushed
for her, and buried her face in Lucinda's neck. The bigger
child drew the smaller one down on her lap and then the fun
began. Uncle Earle gave out the presents, and what presents

they were! Mrs. Gilligan had baked a pound cake for Lucinda; Johanna had made her a pink satin handkerchief case. Mr. Night Owl had brought her Palmer Cox's new Brownie Book. There were dozens of others; besides all of Lucinda's presents for her friends. She had written a verse for every one, and Uncle Earle read them. The only ones Lucinda ever remembered were the ones that went with Trinket's red mittens and Mr. Gilligan's pipe and tobacco:

> *Merry Christmas to Trinket,*
> *These red mittens say.*
> *We'll keep warm her hands*
> *When she goes out to play.*

And to Mr. Gilligan:

> *'Tis a grand thing to be Irish,*
> *And to have an Irish pipe.*
> *May it never need a filling,*
> *May it never need a light.*

Lucinda explained that she knew pipe and light didn't rhyme very well but she hoped Mr. Gilligan wouldn't mind.

There is always one Christmas that belongs to you more than any other—belongs by right of festival and those secret feelings that are never spoken aloud. This Christmas belonged to Lucinda in this way, and I think it belonged to many of her friends. I know it was the only Christmas the Browdowskis kept everlastingly green in their hearts.

As the party was breaking up—Mr. Gilligan having to get

back to his fares—Uncle Earle put thumb and forefinger into his breast pocket rumbling out something about forgetting. "Always carry these with me for the children at Christmas. Just got three left!" And into the pocket of Lucinda's best pinafore, into a pocket of Tony's Sunday clothes, and into one of Trinket's red Christmas mittens went a gold-piece.

"Bless me, don't thank me," said Uncle Earle. "I just go down to the bank the day before Christmas and ask for a pocketful to give away. And they're always nice about it."

As a party it had Aunt Emily's beaten hollow, so Lucinda told Miss Nettie. Miss Peters let Lucinda keep the tree until Twelfth Night, and every day until January 6, Trinket came down at dusk, and she and Lucinda watched the burning candles, and talked softly together about the first time Trinket had seen it. "Long as we live, Trinket, we'll remember this Christmas—a four-year-old Christmas for you and a ten-year-old Christmas for me."

December 7th, 189—

Things begin to look very black for me. How can I have both
The Tempest and Christmas on one dollar a week, car fare
included? Miss Peters calls it a problem in arithmetic and
you can make up your mind when arithmetic gets into your
life trouble comes along with it.

I just have to earn some money. I thought of asking Tony's
father if I could mind the fruit stand for ten cents an afternoon. But I knew what Miss Peters would say to that. Especially as I would have to write it down on my pad. I thought
of asking Louis Sherry if he couldn't let me sell candies in his
place. But I guess I must find a more inconspicuous way. (Inconspicuous is a new word.)

December 10th.

Excelsior! I am saved! I've got me two earning jobs and I love
them both. I take Pygmalion out for an hour and I teach the
Princess English for an hour, and eat Turkish paste, and giggle a lot, and they pay well. So now I can make out my Christmas list a la Jay Gould.

Tony—a jack-knife (his has only one blade.)

Mr. Gilligan—a clay pipe and tobacco.

Johanna—a kitchen apron (Miss Nettie is going to
    sew it for me on the machine.)

Mrs. Gilligan—a tomato pin-cushion.

Uncle Earle—I don't know yet.

Mr. Night-Owl—a cake of soap.

Miss Lucy, honey—some rushing (she wears it.)
The Miss Peterses—handkerchiefs.
Jerry Hanlon—Gum—he chews it.
Trinket—red mittens.
Mrs. B.—bed-slippers. (Miss Nettie will crochet them
    and I buy the wool.)
Mr. B.—a woolen muffler.

I am spreading on the B's; things being as they are but not
mentioned.

                                        December 25th.
Trinket has her red sled! Everybody is as happy as I am—at
least almost. Miss Lucy had an elegant Christmas dinner and
we all went—the B's too. Then we all sang more carols. Johanna brought me a glass ship inside a glass bottle. It's wonderful to think how it got there.

CHAPTER VII

TWELFTH NIGHT

THREE times was the scenery painted for *The Tem-pest*; three times it was thrown into the waste-basket. Tony and Lucinda had spent precious evenings slathering their brushes into paints, pointing them on the tips of their tongues until tongues ran with greens and blues, aquamarines and yellows; and what they brought forth was not right.

After the third attempt Tony spoke his mind plainly, though politely. "Lucinda, I think the scenery, all of it, better be left to me. I make the pictures; you make the costumes and the play. Too many cooks spoil the risotto—yes?"

He tramped up to the Metropolitan Museum of Art on a free day and spent hours sketching any sort of tree, rock, sea that might belong to an enchanted island. He came back to Lucinda treading on air. Now there would be scenery!

And there was. The boy breathed into his fingers all his sense of beauty and imagination. To have tools to work with —a place to work, that was as much as a king could ask; or an artist. He haunted the carriage factory by the river, where they threw out scraps of wood, and brought back chucks, strips, moldings. These found refuge in the Misses Peters' work-room, which stretched itself to hold always a little more. From Christmas on not a moment was wasted. Tony painted and whittled; Miss Nettie and Lucinda sewed; Miss Peters was chief critic and helped Lucinda boil down the play to a proper length, and then listened to her giving a proper reading to the lines. She taught Lucinda something invaluable one night when she said: "Slowly, go more slowly. If a play, a book, a story is worth sharing at all it is worth giving time to."

So Lucinda stopped her eager galloping and gave the lines their full flavor. Without setting herself the task of memorizing she knew nearly the whole of the play by heart before Twelfth Night. She fell into Shakespearean English as easily as she had fallen into Galway brogue. Without being at all conscious of it she regaled the teachers at Miss Brackett's, and Miss Brackett, herself, with such full-flavored expres-

sions as: "Me . . . my library was dukedom large enough."
Or, "For this, be sure, tonight thou shalt have cramps, Side
stitches that shall pen thy breath up." And more than all else
she loved: "What a pied ninny's this, thou scurvy patch!"

She and Uncle Earle were reading *As You Like It* now on
Saturdays, and she brought to him two speeches that rolled
deliciously on her tongue: " 'A pox o' your throat, you bawl-
ing, blasphemous, incharitable dog.' What does a pox o'
your throat mean, Uncle Earle?" And following that— " 'If
thou more murmur'st, I will rend an oak, And peg thee in his
knotty entrails, till Thou hast howl'd away twelve winters.'
It sounds simply elegant but I'm afraid I don't understand it."

Uncle Earle explained and voiced a protest so unnatural
that it flew past Lucinda's ear without even perching there.
"You might leave 'entrails' out of it and say 'insides,' though
why, I don't know. Entrails is a good Anglo-Saxon word,
and we all have them."

The night before, everything was ready. Tony had whittled the ship to be wrecked, made its masts and deck-rails,
and Miss Nettie had made sails for it. Out of soft wood he
had carved an amazing Caliban, a warped and monstrous
creature with thrust-out head and brutish face. He had borrowed some liquid-shoe polish from his friend the bootblack
on Eighth Avenue and stained Caliban a savage brown. It
was Tony's and Lucinda's intention that Caliban should not
be spoiled by so much as a rag of clothing; but Miss Nettie
objected violently to his going naked. She called it "un-
clothed." So she cut up a tan kid glove and they spotted it
with black and hung over Caliban's shoulders a leopard skin.

Ariel was dressed in tiny green wings, patterned after a

lunar moth's; the nymphs wore blue; Miranda had a dress of rose velvet trimmed with Christmas tinsel. Lucinda herself had bearded the men, bringing back from the barber's some little packages of salvaged hair. She had gone there to have her own clipped. She covered the dolls' chins with glue, stuck on the hair, and Miss Nettie trimmed them with her nail-scissors.

It was Miss Nettie who thought of the new theatre curtains, to be made out of the length of old gold plush that had been discarded from Lucinda's own parlor. She made them with little brass rings sewed to the back, with cords to raise and loop them like real stage curtains. Tony painted an asbestos curtain, not real but a satisfactory imitation. Out of flat stones and plaster-of-paris they made Prospero's cave; and Black Sarah gave Lucinda a cupful of cornmeal out of which to strew "these yellow sands."

Nothing went wrong; not a fly in the ointment, Mr. Night-Owl pointed out. At seven-thirty the audience was assembled downstairs in Miss Lucy's drawing-room. The theatre had been put on the largest table and around it draped a portière that Miss Lucy had dug out of a trunk in the attic. Lucinda explained this was very important. Without it her's and Tony's legs would show, and that would have spoiled the whole effect. The theatre had been raised slightly up from the table on a layer of books. In front, on the table, stood a straight row of five bulls-eye lanterns. They were small and new and stank abominably before the evening was over. They faced what Lucinda insisted on calling the proscenium arch; and they made beautiful footlights.

The occupants of Miss Lucy's two houses came as one

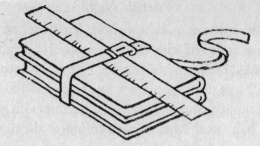

man. Lucinda had invited Mr. Gideon from the church because of the Christmas chocolates, and Dr. Collyer, because he had christened her; but she wasn't sure in her own mind whether the minister and warden of any church should go to a play. It might take their minds off God. Aunt Ellen Douglas and Uncle Tom McCord came; they brought a basket of flowers to present at the dropping of the final curtain. Lucinda had coaxed Uncle Earle to bring the Swiss music-box from Aunt Emily's parlor, secretly and quietly. Lucinda received it with grateful arms. "I hope she won't snoop around tonight and miss it. You see I need it for the music that plays at the beginning and between the acts." She was very eager and serious and excited; and she had been unable to eat any supper.

Tony was to manage Prospero, Ferdinand, the king, Gonzalo, who had been added at the last moment, the boatswain, pronounced as such, Caliban, the nymphs, and the mariners. Lucinda had the master of the ship, Miranda, Ariel, Ceres, and the false duke. Tony ran the music-box; she played the guitar and sang Ariel's songs. Honors were evenly divided except that Lucinda read the play. She wrote in her diary that the moment that Tony turned off the music-box and she pulled up the curtain was the most tremendous in her life.

Compared with other performances of the theatre this was as a crown jewel to a brass ring out of a Christmas cracker.

Of course there had to be a pause—plenty of pause, when Ariel sang a song. Lucinda would reach for the guitar, sit down on the hassock that was also behind the table, sing, and put the guitar back again. But considering everything there was little hitching.

There was one terrible moment in which the audience nearly brought an end to the performance by behaving out of all bounds. Uncle Earle made booming sounds like a muffled drum; and Mr. Night Owl started to whoop with laughter, then thought better of it and choked. Two or three of the ladies gave little gasps of something-or-other. It happened when Lucinda sang the song of the drunken butler because she thought it had such a lovely swing to it. She had found music to go with it out of Walter Crane's "Pan-Pipes," and she had looked forward to the singing of it as one of the high spots in the play. It went in this wise:

> "The master, the swabber, the boatswain, and I,
>   The gunner and his mate,
>   Loved Moll, Meg, and Marian, and Margery,
>   But none of us cared for Kate;
>   For she had a tongue with a tang,
>   Would cry to a sailor, Go hang!
>   She loved not the savour of tar nor of pitch;
>   Yet a tailor might scratch her wher'er she did itch.
>   Then to sea, boys, and let her go hang!"

Lucinda ignored the Epilogue and contented herself with

Prospero's last speech. She might have been addressing her
own audience, and dismissing herself as well as Ariel, as she
spoke the lines with grave solemnity:

> "*I'll deliver all;*
> *And promise you calm seas, auspicious gales,*
> *And sails so expeditious, that shall catch*
> *Your royal fleet afar off.—My Ariel, chick,*
> *That is thy charge: then to the elements*
> *Be free, and fare thou well!*"

Everybody clapped and clapped; and then they came to
look the theatre over, to wonder at the scenery, the actors, the
properties. Lucinda was too young to guess; but here were
men and women who as children had cried out to do this
very thing. And all the desire for it, the disappointment at
never having done it, brought them crowding, eager, rather
wistful, around the children and the theatre that was so small
and held so much.

Lucinda told exuberantly of their doing it all over again
the next night down at the Gedney House. Uncle Earle drew
her aside and whispered a fierce command in her ear. "I don't
like playing Aunt Emily to you, but the song of the drunken
butler, out it goes. You understand—you're not to sing it
again."

"But Uncle Earle, it's an elegant song."

"For a drunken butler, perhaps, but not for you." And
then he threw back his head and roared. "I'd have given a
guinea to have had your Aunt Emily here tonight and seen
her face when you sang it."

Lucinda and Tony took the theatre down to the Gedney House in Mr. Gilligan's hansom cab. The Spindlers had a music-box, so all went well. The princess and Bluebeard came as Mr. and Mrs. Isaac Grose. Mrs. Caldwell came, and Aleda with her grandparents. A few other carefully selected guests filled the manager's parlor. Of course, it was a "repeat" and repeats never went so well as original performances, so said Lucinda. "You see it's real the first time. After that you begin to wonder."

Aleda's grandmother protested, "What would you do if you were an actress and had to repeat not one night but hundreds?"

"I wouldn't. I'd give a new play every night."

"What if you forgot your lines?"

"I'd make them up," said Lucinda.

There was a regular party afterwards. The waiters brought up ice cream and ladyfingers and meringues. Everybody thought the way Tony had carved the ship and Caliban was remarkable. Lucinda drew Mr. Spindler aside: "I wish you'd give him a place in your hotel. You see the Coppinos are full up with children—Liza and Pietro and Gemma and Tessa and I don't know how many more. There's always a new one every time I go. Tony ought not to spend his life at a fruit-stand, especially when he can make such lovely things with his hands. Do think about it, please, Mr. Spindler."

Snow came, and more snow. Lucinda gradually became boxed up, taking the horse-car to school every day with Miss Peters; spending afternoons indoors. So did the lid of the box begin to press down upon her, she could feel it fastened, holding her there. Would nothing happen, would nobody slip the hook and let her pop out? Inevitably there came a week of disgrace. It began with a call at Louis Sherry's. He was not at his shop, but the young lady behind the confectionery knew what would have happened had he been there. She filled a paper bag with Lucinda's favorite candies. Then on to Brackett's and the bag with temptation was put into her desk; the lid was closed over them with the best intenions to keep them there. Study-hour came, and Miss Benton, the prettiest and the youngest of all the teachers, strolled out of the room. It was too lucky a chance to throw away. Out came Louis Sherry, up and down the aisles went the bag, without let or hindrance. Every mouth was stuffed full as in came, not Miss Benton—but Anna C. Brackett. Every head bent over its desk but Alberta's. Alberta was too bland, too witless, too smothered with contentment. She stared at Miss Brackett, mild in the eye, and chewed her candy with the complacency of a cow.

"Alberta!"

Alberta rose.

"Come here!"

Alberta came—or went; at any rate she arrived at the front of the room and Miss Brackett. Lucinda was wishing that Alberta would swallow the candy and choke herself on it.

"What are you chewing?"

Alberta opened her mouth for convenience and displayed, smeared over her tongue, the remnants of what had been a chocolate nougatine.

"Where did you get it?"

Again, conveniently, Alberta nodded towards Lucinda.

Miss Brackett came down the aisle, stopping by Lucinda's

desk. By this time she was fully aware that every mouth was occupied. "Lucinda, where did you get candy?"

Lucinda overstepped her mark. She tried to be altogether too friendly at the wrong moment. She dove into her desk, brought out the bag, said with a grand manner: "From my friend, Louis Sherry. Have one, Miss Brackett."

Severely the bag was removed from Lucinda's possession. It went into the pocket of Miss Brackett's muslin apron; she wore one in school always over a blue-and-white print dress. "This is the first time you've broken a rule in school, Lucinda. Don't let it happen again."

Lucinda did not break another rule. She did something far worse before the week was out. So heinous a crime it was, that no pupil was thought capable of committing it; hence no rule had ever been made to prevent it. How the idea came to Lucinda I cannot remember; she was suddenly taken with it, and found it completely wicked and enchanting.

Every pupil in the school had fastened to the lid of her desk with thumb-tacks her study schedule. It ran in this wise:

Thursday

9:00   Arithmetic 4 — Room G.
10:00   French 2   — Room A.
11:00   Study-Hour   — Room H.

On the stroke of the first gong in the downstairs hall— every pupil in every room rose, books in hand; on the second stroke they filed out in perfect order, column passing column in the hall in silence; each class going systematically to the room assigned it. What would happen, Lucinda wondered, if everybody went to a different room! Arriving twenty minutes early one day at the end of the week, there was ample time to change the schedules on every desk and find out what would happen.

On the stroke of the second gong came a pandemonium that had never before occurred on Thirty-Ninth Street. In the hallways, big, little, and middle-sized girls jumbled together, forgot the rule of silence and broke out into wild bleatings. Rooms were in an uproar. It was half an hour before order was restored. Miss Brackett marshaled the shattered ranks like a splendid color-sergeant. After that she came straight for Lucinda.

Lucinda had opened her Cornelius Nepos and was going through the motions of translating. She tried to turn up to Miss Brackett an eye of innocence. But what was the use? Miss Brackett was like God—you couldn't fool her.

"Did you do it?"

"Yes, Miss Brackett."

"Go downstairs; put on your things and leave the school. Don't come back until I send for you."

Lucinda was prepared for anything but this. The old Lucinda had learned to take punishment, chin-up; sermons had been preached at her since her ears had been open. She had been kept home from parties, deprived of her allowance, sent to bed supperless, and had worn a placard on certain days telling of her sins. But all this had happened to the old Lucinda, the Lucinda without roller skates, fastened into her box. Yet even the old Lucinda had never been sent home from school.

She was dumbfounded—humiliated. The misery was like a rock in her stomach. Her feet dragged her down the stairs, into the coat-room, out the door. She found herself at last on the corner of Bryant Park, and Patrolman M'Gonegal was casting a puzzled eye at her: "A grand day to you, Miss. How's living?"

"Rotten. Mr. M'Gonegal, I think you ought to put me in jail."

"Talking of jail, are you? What have you done? Stolen the mayor's badge?"

Lucinda could feel her head hang heavy, almost to her boot-tops. "I've been deliberately bad. Lots of times I'm bad when I don't plan to be. But this was deliberate. What do policemen do to a little girl my age who's been sent away from school?"

Patrolman M'Gonegal was at his wit's end. "We've never had a case as bad as that. I might send in a call for the Black Maria and give you a day in jail. But if I did, like as not, the judge would give me another. Have you a friend, hereabouts, handy?"

Lucinda suddenly brightened. She had lots of friends at the Gedney House, two blocks off. She explained this to the policeman.

"Good. Consider yourself arrested. March yourself around to the friend you like best and lock yourself up till noon." He waved her off with his billy high in the air. And Lucinda went, feeling better.

Her feet still dragged, but her mind skipped ahead. She would stop first and see her adored Princess Zayda; then she would go up to Mrs. Caldwell and make a free confession of all she had done. After that she would give Pygmalion a free airing; he deserved it because of the red sled.

At suite 207 she hesitated. Would she knock first, or just

go in softly and give the princess an immense surprise? She decided against knocking. The door made no noise; she edged in quietly and closed it after her. She had never visited the princess in the morning. It seemed funny to find all daylight shut out and the hanging lamps burning. The strangeness of it halted Lucinda's progress. She stopped and listened. Not a sound. Where was the princess? Where was the oriental servant?

Walking softly across the small square of hallway she stood looking through the portières into the parlor. She could see the figure of her princess crushed among the cushions on the divan. Was she asleep? It was still early in the morning. Maybe ladies from Asia didn't get up early. Could she be crying? But there was no sound of crying.

Lucinda took one step inside the room and shouted "Boo!" or at least she thought she shouted it. It sounded in that still room no louder than a breath. She did better the second time. There followed a crescendo of boos: "Boo! Boo! Boo! ! !" That ought to wake the whole hotel! It woke nobody. There was no stirring of the figure; no voice saying: "How veree nice!"

On the toes of her stubby boots Lucinda walked to the divan. She did not want to walk there; she wanted to climb back into her box and have somebody fasten the lid safely down on her. But walk she did, seeing things as she went: the Japanese doll she had named Nanky Pu was on the floor; the princess was lying with her face buried in the cushions; she was wearing the loveliest gown she had even seen her wear, all flowing gold and crimson, and in the back of it stood, straight up, the jeweled hilt of the dagger that should have been hanging on the wall. Lucinda's eyes fled to the spot where it had always hung. It was empty.

Did the servant know about this? Did Mr. Isaac Grose know? Where were they? What should she do? She must tell somebody—somebody quickly. Halfway across the room she stopped and looked back. She couldn't leave Nanky Pu that way on the floor. She went back, picked him up and laid him gently beside the princess. She went as quietly as she had come, but once beside the stairs she tore up them, two flights, to the rooms of Mr. Spindler. She beat with hard fists on the door. She wanted to scream but knew she mustn't.

The look on Mrs. Spindler's face at such a knocking changed. Lucinda watched it change as she threw her arms about Mrs. Spindler's middle and dragged her into the room. In a voice that didn't sound like her own she said: "Please send for Mr. Spindler—quick!"

The manager came, and all of a sudden Lucinda found she couldn't tell him anything. She sat on Mrs. Spindler's lap and sniveled, and the sniveling grew to a blubbering, and the blubbering to a torrent of crying. The manager drew his chair close to Mrs. Spindler's. He stroked Lucinda's hand and left her free to cry it out. It stopped the way it had begun, in snivels. Then Lucinda told.

She had to go over it twice, very slowly. Suddenly it seemed as if Mr. Spindler was afraid—afraid for her. He questioned her very closely. Had anybody seen her going in or out of the suite? Lucinda was sure nobody had. Who had seen her coming into the hotel? Only Charlie, the doorman. She had walked up the stairs. There were people in the lobby but nobody she knew. Had she dropped anything in Mrs. Grose's room? No, she had nothing to drop. She was puzzled about all these questions. She wanted the manager to go back to the room—to go quickly—to do something for the princess.

Mr. Spindler took both her hands and held them so tight they hurt.

"Listen, Lucinda, something very ugly, very terrible has happened in that room. I don't want you mixed up in it. There is nothing I can do. If I go down there now the police will ask me—why did you go? And I will have to say, because a little girl named Lucinda Wyman went there first. That mustn't happen. Do you understand?"

"Not quite," said Lucinda.

"Then you must take my word for it. You must trust me. Mrs. Grose has been killed. There is nothing we can do to help her now. But I know she would not want you troubled about it. Pretty soon one of the maids will go in to make the beds. She will be the one to find out what has happened. She will come to me and tell me, and then I will call for the police. I will say the maid found her when she went in."

He stood up, put on his hat and coat, took Lucinda's hand. "We're going out. Remember, in case you are asked any questions that you came to see me about that Italian boy who is such a good friend of yours. I think, perhaps, I can do something for him."

They took the elevator downstairs and walked out on Broadway. Outside it occurred to Mr. Spindler to ask why she wasn't in school. Lucinda told the whole miserable story. "Well, you can't go back to the boarding house. You mustn't be alone—not now. You'd be thinking about it. Let's see what we can do."

Lucinda made up her mind in an instant. "I'd like to spend the day with Mrs. Gilligan." She had a picture of Mrs. Gilligan's ample lap, of griddle bread with currants in it, of a small tidy kitchen with geraniums blooming there, of how much Mrs. Gilligan might have looked like Johanna when she was young. "If you don't mind waiting till Mr. Gilligan happens by, I know he'd take me down."

So they waited, walking slowly, Mr. Spindler explaining that what had happened must never be told to anyone. Lucinda must forget all about it; she must make believe it had never happened; she must think of her princess as suddenly going away, back to her own country. "You'll do just that, Lucinda. I'm depending on you." He was smiling down at her as Mr. Gilligan drove into view, without a fare.

"I'll try; I'll try very hard," Lucinda promised this as she climbed into the cab. Mr. Spindler insisted on paying her fare down and explained that she had been rather a naughty girl in school for which she was very sorry, and would the Gilligans look after her until late afternoon.

The Gilligans would, and did. Mrs. Gilligan clucked over her like the hen with one chick. Lucinda made the griddle bread, and Mr. Gilligan pronounced it the best he had ever eaten. After he had gone forth with the cab again, Mrs. Gilligan offered the ample lap and Lucinda crept into it like any lost chicken. Back to Ireland they went, the two of them, to County Kerry and County Wicklow, to fairy raths and fairy pipers, to the song of the shee and the deeds of the brave men. Lucinda did a humiliating thing; she went to sleep with her head on Mrs. Gilligan's shoulder in the middle of the tale of Fionn MacCumal and the Salmon of Wisdom. She never woke until Mr. Gilligan came back to fetch her. She was so ashamed. She hadn't gone to sleep in anybody's lap since she had been Trinket's size.

All the way driving home to Miss Lucy's brownstone front, Lucinda wondered what Miss Peters would say, and Miss Peters said nothing. She did not act shocked as mam'selle would have, or grieved like mama. She acted perfectly natural —as if nothing between them had happened that really mattered.

Only into Lucinda's diary went the thing that really mattered, and after she had written she locked the desk and tied the key again around her neck under her nightgown. She would wear it night and day until mama came home to make it safe.

January 14th, 189—

It has been a hellious day. It never seemed terrible when you read the Arabian Nights and Fatima plunged the dagger into Ali Baba. I never want to read another story about a dagger. I never want to go back to the Gedney House again. I never want to go back to Miss Brackett's. I want spring to come. I want to put on my roller skates and skate far off to some place I have never been before.

Good-bye my Princess—my dear, dear Princess Zayda. I hope you are safely back in your tower and that the Prince is going to find you there.

ROLLER SKATES

THE snow held through February into March. Before
the pavements were shoveled clean, fresh snow fell.
There was hardly an afternoon that Lucinda could not take

Trinket out on the red sled; and hardly a night when she did not bring her in to have supper on the cutting table, with the dolls' dishes. Lucinda sang a constant song from the *Saint Nicholas Song Book:*

> *"Oh, I wish the winter would go;*
> *And I wish the summer would come;*
> *Then the Big Brown Farmer would hoe,*
> *And the Little Brown Bee would hum*
>   *Ho-hum!"*

Trinket would end the verse with her: "Ho-hum!" Lucinda had numberless promises for her that had to do with spring. These were vague to Trinket, but because Lucinda wanted so plainly to have spring come it held to reason that Trinket wanted it too. "Pussy-willows out in the Park, and the red japonica bushes in bloom; oh, Trinket, red as fire. And the swan boats back on the pond. We'll ride in them. We'll be having rhubarb and strawberries soon for supper instead of prunes. Think of that! And I'll be getting out my roller skates."

But spring dilly-dallied. Then came a night as Lucinda lay awake in her folding bed, both windows open, when there was something in the wind, something startlingly different. Snow still banked the streets but for all of that Lucinda sniffed under and beyond the reach of the snow and smelled new life in the air. She had never been conscious of smelling spring before it came; it made her tingle down her back and wriggle her toes between the sheets in a strange, new excitement. If she had Pegasus to ride through the night, she would ride straight south, catch up spring and bear it citywards like a blossoming branch. Oh, to have Bellerophon's enchanted bridle to catch Pegasus with! Anyway, she had her roller skates. Out they'd come in the morning and away she would go to school. She could tell Miss Brackett her troubles were over. Soon the whole world would be full of roller skates and robins again.

Overnight the thaw came, and sure enough out of the wardrobe came the skates. It seemed a year since the day Lucinda had been sent away from school; it seemed a hundred years since she had waved good-bye to Miss Peters at the curb and had gone clump—chug—chirr—clump to her freedom.

Almost she might have crested an empty world that morning for she was not conscious of any other living soul on Fifth Avenue. Arms swinging, her winter felt bonnet edging off her head, her skates beating aloud a rhythm that got into her head and bones. It set itself to poetry and Lucinda chanted aloud—a verse to a block—oblivious of the amused, amazed faces that turned to watch her swing by them:

"Over in the meadow in the sand, in the sun,
  Lived an old mother toad and her little toadie one.
  'Blink,' said the mother. 'I blink,' said the one;
  So they winked and they blinked in the sand, in the sun."

To her abounding delight the poem lasted till she reached Thirty-Ninth Street and she turned the corner on "The wise mother ant and her little anties twelve."

Imperfect fractions that day performed fandangoes; his

tory dates tumbled about like clowns; her translation of *Sans Famille* bounded about like a rambunctious goat. And just as school was getting over and done with Miss Brackett came into the room and demanded of her: "Who is the young man downstairs waiting for you?"

"I wonder!" said Lucinda. Then she caught a queer look on Miss Brackett's face and answered with more respect. "I truly don't know. I can't think of a single young man I know except Edward MacDowell, and he wouldn't bother about me."

"We'll go downstairs and find out."

They did, and it was Mr. Night Owl. It was the day for Barnum and Bailey's Circus parade. He had come to take her, afraid she might miss it. Lucinda begged to go back and get Trinket. "Please, Mr. Night Owl. Probably it will be her first circus parade, just as Christmas was her first tree."

So back they went for Trinket; and away went the three of them to Madison Avenue. There were still snowdrifts, and they had to climb them to see over into the street. Trinket insisted on sitting down, and Lucinda got leg-ache; so Mr. Night Owl bought some newspapers and spread them triple-thick on the soggy drift.

It was a wonderful parade, although none of the hot country animals were in it, like camels and elephants and holy cows. But there were floats picturing all the fairy-tales: The Sleeping Beauty and Little Red Riding Hood, Ali Baba and his Forty Thieves, Cinderella and Aladdin. Trinket crowed with delight, and such a clapping of hands they made between them!

For Saturday afternoon Mr. Night Owl got three press

seats to see the circus perform under the new flying Diana on Madison Square Garden. Lucinda rushed up to the third floor to borrow Trinket for that and found Mrs. Browdowski at the door, looking worried. "She has a cold, Lucinda. Trinket's in bed; she can't go."

So they took Tony instead; and Mr. Night Owl was sure it had turned out better that way. There were lots of things in a circus that might have frightened such a little girl. They all went to have lunch at Purssell's. Lucinda favored Purssell's. She knew Gustave, the cross-eyed head waiter, and the excellence of the Bath buns. "We go there often when mama and I go shopping. It's sort of a reward for me when I'm good and mama shops hours for guimp."

"What's guimp?"

"I don't know. It comes by the yard wound up on a big piece of pasteboard."

"Well, let's take Purssell's this time without guimp."

They did, and sat on the stools round the big oval counter. Gustave remembered Lucinda for all that she hadn't been

there for so long and asked after "Madame," and assured her
that the Bath buns were excellent as always. Lucinda ordered
a chicken patty, a Bath bun, and a cup of hot chocolate with
whipped cream. "I always do, because I never can think of
anything better. I always hope I'm going to have room for
ice cream but I never have. The Bath bun fills me up to the
gills." Tony ordered what she did and watched her every
movement. Afterwards with hands hard locked in the ecstasy
of anticipation they walked together over to Madison Square.
Lucinda stubbed her toe frequently and would have fallen
had not the Night Owl and Tony held firmly to her hands.
And this was because she could never cross Madison Square
without tilting her head far back to see the magnificent new
tower on it, and Diana on tiptoe, bending her bow, to speed
its arrow across the city. "I love Diana," said Lucinda, stubbing her toe again. "She's the goddess, defending the city.
I hope she'll be there forever."

Inside the smell was heavenly—of the tan-bark, freshly
sprinkled, of the animals, hot peanuts, and popcorn. Half the
circus was the smell of it. They were hunting for their seats
when a man in a tall hat said: "Press seats? Your name, Sir?"

Mr. Night Owl said it was Hugh Marshall.

"Paper?"

"*New York Sun.*"

He looked down with interest at Lucinda. "Who's the
young lady?"

"She's my young lady—Lucinda."

"Well, we're looking for somebody to ride Jumbo. In the
howdah, y' know. Think you'd like to be a passenger?"

Would she! She squeezed Mr. Night Owl's hand hard

to signify her willingness; and said urgently, "Thank you, couldn't we all go?"

"Why not? Follow that aisle. It'll take you back to the costume stalls. Just say you're riding Jumbo and they'll give you cloaks and turbans. Have to keep up the oriental splendor, y' know."

"Hurrah! We're going to have oriental splendor. Come on, Tony. Come on, Mr. Night Owl." Lucinda tugged and pulled them after her. As the reporter confessed afterwards, no one could have hired him for that show except Lucinda.

Lucinda was given a pair of red satin trousers that she could pull over everything she had on, a golden tunic and a red turban with a gold crescent on it. Her wide, black eyes spun threads of excitement that gathered in all those about them. "Do I look truly oriental? Will I look like a lady of the harem riding out to kill tigers or jaguars or whatever they ride out on elephants for?" Years afterwards when she was to read for the first time Kipling's *Just So Stories* she was to say over to herself very slowly, remembering:

"There lived a Parsee from whose hat the rays of the sun were reflected with more than oriental splendor."

Tony wore a yellow cloak and turban; Mr. Night Owl wore blue satin with gold. They were told where to stand; and when Jumbo lumbered down the run-way Lucinda held her breath so long she thought she would never get it back again. It seemed as if there never could be such another elephant living: with the red and gold howdah on his back, the red and gold cuffs on his huge legs, the long velvet saddle-

cloth, tasseled with gold, and the mahout on his head, wield
ing the great gold ankus. "It's much too elegant for us," whispered Lucinda, "Diana ought to be riding instead."

But she climbed the ladder held against Jumbo's side. She
was shown where to sit and Tony and Mr. Night Owl took
their places beside her, hands locked.

The grand opening procession began. Outriders on black
horses with long-stemmed trumpets tooted a fanfare. The
band, in their red and gold uniforms struck up such music
as had never been heard by a lady of the harem before; Lucinda was sitting up so high she could almost have reached
the moon. The howdah rocked like a ship at sea. "Lucky I'm
a tiptop sailor or I'd be ruining everything," she thought.
Aloud she and Tony never spoke until the parade was over;
until she had gone all the way around the huge amphitheatre
and watched Arabs and Egyptians, giraffes and monkey-
ridden ponies, bareback riders and clowns, lion cages and
snake charmers follow after her. But bow she did—to that
vast audience, and fluttered the feather fan they had given
her at all the children.

She climbed down the ladder from Jumbo, fed him a bag
of peanuts, took off her red satin trousers, and thanked the
wardrobe mistress as well as the man in the high hat. Not
until they were in their seats, close to the tan-bark, and every
one of the three big rings had claimed its performers, did she
speak: "Mr. Night Owl, I'm going to tell my children about
this some day when their father and I take them to the circus.
They probably won't believe me but that doesn't matter."

Afterwards they visited the animals, saw the midgets, and
shook hands with Mr. Tom Thumb. The lamp-lighters were

touching off the city, making avenues to shine north and south, streets, east and west, like a huge lighted checkerboard. Lucinda clutched the hand of Mr. Night Owl. "I bet you that Diana gets a whale of a view at night from way up there. Wouldn't you like to be her—once?"

"Not on your tintype. It's bad enough tackling night in New York on solid ground. What would I do with fires and brawls and night-courts, suspended a quarter of the way up to heaven?"

"You'd see more," said Lucinda practically, "but you wouldn't get 'round so fast."

Every day, for half a week, Lucinda knocked gently on the Browdowski door to ask after Trinket; no pounding of fists or shouting now. Each time Mrs. Browdowski stood blocking the opening; or Mr. Browdowski slipped through the half-opened door and closed it behind him to give Lucinda some message from Trinket. They were still hiding their poverty behind their strong, young bodies. Each of them answered Lucinda the same, and with brave lips: "She's just got a cold, Lucinda. We're keeping her quiet and in bed."

"Have you had a doctor?" Lucinda asked one day.

"Oh, no. She isn't sick enough for a doctor."

"Maybe you'd better, just the same." Lucinda believed in doctors; at least she believed in Doctor Hitchcock—kind, unfailing, and so wise. What she did not know was that you paid doctors to come and see you; that part of Doctor Hitchcock's service had never come under her notice.

A late Thursday afternoon it was and she climbed the stairs again to ask for Trinket. Trinket's father opened the door, his hair jumping about on top of his head as if whipped there by his fine, nervous fingers. His lips weren't brave to-day. He looked at Lucinda a little doubtfully and said: "No better. But you have always been a good doctor, yes. Perhaps if you came in for a few minutes . . ."

So in Lucinda went, and sat on the edge of the big bed so she could be beside Trinket's crib. She made clown-faces for Trinket, who laughed in a funny, croaking little voice. "I think she doesn't look sick at all. I never saw her cheeks so red or her eyes so bright." Lucinda was very positive about it. "Couldn't I borrow her tonight for supper—right out of her crib—bedclothes and all? You could carry her down and put her on my bed. Just give me a jiffy to get it opened."

They looked at each other—Trinket's father and mother, and then Trinket's father said: "Why not?" And Trinket's mother said: "She might eat something if she was having supper with you, Lucinda. For days she hasn't eaten any more than a canary bird."

So Lucinda clumped downstairs and threw back the curtains and pulled down the bed and shook up the pillows and patted them smooth and had everything ready when Mr. Browdowski brought Trinket down.

Miss Nettie came in soon after and together they brought in the cutting table and laid it, and while Miss Nettie got milk-toast ready, and prunes, and cocoa, and cut sponge cake thick and chunky, Lucinda told about the circus and the wonderful ride on Jumbo's back.

With supper on, Lucinda sat on the edge of the bed and coaxed every mouthful down Trinket's little red lane. She made up an exciting game about it that made Trinket smile every time she played it over again.

"Jumbo's hungry. You've got to eat some milk-toast for Jumbo," and Trinket would open her mouth and down would go one spoonful.

"Here comes the monkey—the chattering, jumping monkey!" Lucinda stopped, spoon poised in hand, to chatter, "He didn't get any breakfast today; here's milk-toast for the monkey," and down went another spoonful.

"Now comes the giraffe. He's got the longest legs and the longest neck, and he's all covered over with chocolate spots. He's terribly thirsty!" Down went the doll's cup of cocoa.

"Here comes Mr. Barnum and Mr. Bailey. They take off their top-hats and bow and say: "Please, Trinket, we'd like a little sponge cake and a prune or two.""

So did they eat for the tall clown with the flapping feet, the leader of the circus band with the red coat and the brass braid, the lady in the pink spangled skirts who rode the milk-white horse. With delight, and a certain vainglorious pride Lucinda numbered for Mr. Browdowski the spoonfuls, the cupfuls, the prunes and the half-piece of sponge cake Trinket had eaten.

Next day Lucinda skated 'round to the Coppinos to tell them that her mama and papa were sailing home from Italy in June. And they were bringing presents home. She knew they would love to bring something to the Coppinos. What should it be? She hadn't been there for a long time. To her surprise she found a clothes-basket by the kitchen fire and in it was a new bambino, looking like a fresh-baked loaf of Italian bread, all wound up tight and snug. "Goodness gracious. How did it come—stork or cabbage?"

This was too much for Mrs. Coppino, and Tony, wiser in

babies, turned his back and looked out into the yard. Nowise daunted, Lucinda pursued her inquiry: "Name? What's its name?"

Tony interpreted; Mrs. Coppino answered: "Cesare."

"Cesare—Caesar. Julius Caesar!" Lucinda exploded with joy. She'd be in Caesar next year and the Coppinos had a bambino named for him. It somehow struck her ridiculously funny and she shouted: "No time at all and he'll be dividing all Gaul into three parts," which meant nothing at all to the Coppinos.

She skated back to the Gedney House the next day to tell Mr. Spindler about the new bambino and urge him to think seriously about Tony. "There just isn't room for Tony there any longer. How they all get in now, I don't know. They'll be sleeping the bambinos in orange crates and Tony'll have to hang up like a bunch of bananas."

Mr. Spindler promised to think seriously. Lucinda hadn't been back to the hotel since she had written in her diary her good-bye to the princess. She couldn't bear now to go upstairs. The next day being Saturday, she hoofed it to Aunt Emily's and climbed up to the library. Because of the circus she had missed a week and she was eager to finish *As You Like It* and see what Uncle Earle would choose next. She had loved Touchstone and Phoebe and Jacques; she'd be sorry to get to the end of them. But think of beginning something new! Think of watching Uncle Earle open a new book and read the cast of characters!

When that wonderful moment finally came Uncle Earle sat for a long time, his finger holding open another volume, his eyes searching Lucinda, for all the world, Lucinda thought, as if she had been the new play. At last he said: "So far we've read only comedies. Do you think you are old and wise enough for a tragedy?"

"What's the difference?"

Uncle Earle explained briefly: a comedy was a happy affair wherein all ended well; a tragedy ended with catastrophe —death. There were violent conflicts between people in tragedies; they made mistakes and you followed them through to their bitter endings. "But—" Uncle Earle leaned forward in his chair and rapped the knuckles of his fingers against the book, "in fine tragedies, such as the Greeks and William Shakespeare wrote, what happens must be inevitable—unescapable. It must make you feel right about the ending. And great tragedies must have beauty in them; otherwise what's the use?"

"Inevitable. That's a new word," Lucinda rolled it pleasantly on her tongue.

"It means—" Uncle Earle paused, then went on. "One of the characters in this play, a certain Friar Lawrence, put the meaning neatly into words when he said: "What must be— must be; that's a certain text.""

"I guess I understand."

"I can put it another way, Snoodie. Think of everything that happens in the play as adding up correctly to make the ending. Just as if you were to take 5 and 2 and 6 and should add them up to make 13. Right? Well, that sum was inevitable."

"I get it. What's the play?"

"*Romeo and Juliet*." Uncle Earle read the majestic prologue to it. Lucinda was to carry home with her that line about a pair of star-crossed lovers. She was to wonder, walking slowly, after supper with the gazelles, if a kind of five and two and six had added up right for the princess. That would make it a tragedy, but where was the beauty in it? She remembered the lovely gold and crimson gown she was wearing—that had beauty. And the hilt of the dagger sparkled in a beautiful way; she supposed that dagger was beautiful. And she guessed that the feelings the princess must have had, getting away from Mr. Isaac Grose for good, must have been very, very beautiful.

Katie had to call her twice for supper, so spell-bound was she with this new play. When she went it was with leaden feet, loath to leave behind her the spell of old Verona. She turned at the door to say: "Verona, that's Italy. That's where mama and papa are. It's a real place. You can take a boat and get there. It isn't like Prospero's island. I'm going some day."

It was a rather pleasant supper that night with the gazelles. Aunt Emily was dressing to go out for dinner so she didn't hover. Mam'selle had been called down to do something about the dress, so the five were left alone. And then Agatha and Sybil went off to be by themselves because they were older, and Lucinda suddenly had a splendid idea.

She had been looking hard at Frances and Virginia, and thinking she could do a lot for them—roller skates could do a lot for them—an afternoon free of any watchful eye could do a lot for them. And she came out with the idea as if it had been a bursting bomb: "Let's go to Proctor's—just the three of us."

"Proctor's!" They couldn't have breathed more sin into the word if it had been hell. Lucinda knew why. Aunt Emily

considered Proctor's a low and vulgar theatre where they performed low and vulgar plays in a low and vulgar way.

But she had heard the Solomons say otherwise. Aleda had
gone, and seen an exciting play called *The English Rose*.
You could get into the gallery for twenty-five cents.

Frances and Virginia protested together: "But we couldn't
take twenty-five cents out of our allowances without mama
or mam'selle finding us out."

"Haven't you something you could hock?" This was as
sudden an idea as going to Proctor's. There was a pawn-shop
on Eighth Avenue. Tony had pointed it out with its three
golden balls and had told Lucinda that when you were very
poor and needed money you could take something there and
hock it.

"Hock!" Those two of Aunt Emily's docile daughters had
never heard the word, but it sounded bad to them.

Lucinda explained. She went on to say that she would get
Miss Peters to invite them over for St. Patrick's Day. They
could come home from school with her, spend the afternoon,
and have supper. She thought Miss Peters could manage it
if Frances and Virginia could manage the twenty-five cents
each. "What have you got to hock?" insisted Lucinda.

Books seemed to be the only safe thing. They had any
number of picture books, long since outgrown and as good
as new. Could Lucinda . . .

Lucinda could. She took six of the books home with her.
She routed Tony up before going home and besought him
to do the hocking. He didn't like the idea; but St. Patrick's
Day was Monday—not a moment to lose.

Tony got seventy-five cents for them. Lucinda generously

invited him to go, too, and keep one of the quarters to pay his way in.

The night that finished St. Patrick's Day Lucinda wrote with a fine flourish in her diary.

March 17th, 189—

Well—we went and did it; and Aunt Emily hasn't found out. At least not up to the present moment.

It was a perfectly Elegant play and nobody saw anything vulgar in it. And not a dry moment—as Uncle Earle would say. There was a grand steeplechase in it; only the scenery moved and the horses stood still—wooden horses. Somebody killed somebody beside a place called Devil's Bridge. The gentlemen talked just as politely as Uncle Earle, and the ladies were every bit as careful of their manners as Aunt Emily. The villian got hissed which was pleasant and fun to do. You do it through your teeth. I watched Tony. Among us we made a lot of hissing.

Supper was fun. Tony came. The gazelles like him a lot and wish they could have him 'round their house. We had creamed chicken and English muffins, and ice-cream in the shape of shamrocks, and little frosted cakes with harps on them. If only the two youngest gazelles can keep from telling the two oldest all will be well. But if Sybil and Agatha find out—they'll peach. (Peach, I guess is a vulgar word. It was used in the play and means to tell on you.)

I forgot to write down that somebody is building a tomb for General Grant way out in the country by the river. Everybody is supposed to give towards it. I met papa's friend Seth Milligan skating home from school and I gave him a nickel. Trinket isn't so well.

CHAPTER IX

A GULL FLIES SEAWARD

IT was the next morning that Lucinda asked advice from her friend Patrolman M'Gonegal. Before skating to school she had gone up to the third floor to ask again for Trinket. Mrs. Browdowski came to the door looking unslept and tousled. "She's very sick, Lucinda."

"Haven't you had a doctor yet?"

"No."

"Aren't you going to?"

"I—don't know."

At Forty-Second Street she fell in with Patrolman M'Gonegal and hailed him. "You're not asking to be jailed again, by any chance?" he grinned.

Lucinda shook a doleful head, "No, I wish it was just about me I was bothered. Mr. M'Gonegal, if you had a very precious friend, not much bigger than a pint-pot, and she had been sick for a whole week and longer, and her papa and mama hadn't sent for a doctor, what would you do?"

The policeman removed his hat and scratched his head. "Now that's a tough one. You see, if it was one of mine, I'd be having a doctor in, first thing."

"Do doctors cost money?" This possible enlightenment had come to Lucinda that morning.

"They do that."

"Then that's the trouble. They're dreadfully poor, and dreadfully kind. They wouldn't want to ask a doctor to come and not pay him."

Patrolman M'Gonegal looked at Lucinda as if he knew something was stirring in her mind. "And what were you thinking of doing about it?"

"You see we have a perfectly elegant family doctor. He's cured everyone who's ever been sick in our house and that makes ten, counting upstairs and downstairs. I never saw papa pay him to take care of us, but maybe he does, quietly. I thought if I told him about the Browdowskis he'd want to come anyway."

"I'd talk it over with him," said Patrolman M'Gonegal. "He'd be the lad that could tell you."

After school Lucinda skated straight to Doctor Hitchcock's. He lived on the same block with Aunt Ellen Douglas. She found him at lunch—a late one; and he insisted on her taking the big armchair at the other end of the table and helping him out, as he called it. So she ate a mutton chop and baked potato with him while he told her she looked the despair of any doctor. "Not a sick day since the parents left, I'll be bound, hey?"

"Not a one," agreed Lucinda.

"If more parents would go away and leave their ten-year-olds—or their twelve-to-fifteen-year-olds—I'd be a poor man," and he chuckled.

"It isn't about that I came," explained Lucinda. She had been trying to think of some way to begin. "You're such a kind person, Doctor Hitchcock, about the kindest in the world. Uncle Earle says there isn't anyone who helps people out of it easier."

The doctor's mouth was full of mutton chop, and he let the remark go unchallenged. Lucinda went on, headlong: "You see there's a little girl—a very special little girl dreadfully sick on the third floor where I live with Miss Peters. Her parents are awfully poor. They won't always be for he's going to be a famous person; I mean Trinket's father. But just now they haven't any doctor. I think they haven't sent for one because they know they can't pay him. And if you saw Trinket once you'd feel bothered about her as I do. It's rather a jumble, isn't it?" she ended disgustedly.

Doctor Hitchcock put down his knife and fork and plucked at his beard. "I say, Lucinda, how do you find all these things out about people? What would your mother say to your taking up with strangers? Suppose it's catching!"

"I'm sure it isn't, and they're about my best friends."

"I'd come in a minute; but it isn't as easy as you would

suppose. Just suppose I went there, gave the little girl some medicine, told her parents to do this and that, and then the patient got worse?"

"Oh, but she wouldn't! None of your patients ever get worse."

Doctor Hitchcock chuckled in his beard and mumbled something about sublime faith; but he looked put out when he spoke. "Lots of 'em die. Keep that in your mind."

"I'd rather not," said Lucinda firmly. "Don't you remember the time we had diphtheria, the three of us, and you and mama and Mary O'Brien worked on us, day and night. We didn't die."

"God's mercy—that's all."

"Mama said it was you. Please, Doctor Hitchcock! Somebody's got to look after Trinket. And I should say there wasn't a moment to lose."

Still the doctor plucked his beard. There was that high barrier called Medical Ethics; he could hardly explain it to Lucinda. But no doctor of repute went anywhere until he was called. He went on plucking his beard, just as Patrolman M'Gonegal scratched his head. Thinking seemed to be so much harder work when you grew up. Lucinda found herself wishing she could always stay ten, for ever and ever.

She had finished her mutton chop; she had lost interest in the baked potato. She sat very straight, holding herself up on the arms of the chair so that she could look straighter across the table. "Suppose," she said very slowly, "you didn't come; and Trinket got worse?"

The doctor looked straight back at Lucinda and said: "I'm beaten. When do you want me?"

"Now!"

And *now* it was. Lucinda had a desperate feeling that if she didn't hold fast to Doctor Hitchcock and take him with her he might vanish. So they went around to Miss Lucy's together, skates dangling over Lucinda's back, held there by the straps; and she walked soberly beside the doctor, telling him all the little intimate, private things she knew about the Browdowskis. "Now you'll think of them as old friends, too," she explained.

He sent her up the third flight ahead of him to announce his coming, while he waited below in the Misses Peters' parlor. As she went, Lucinda turned to him a radiant face: "What do you bet Trinket won't be better tomorrow! And if money comes into it at all just you remember I have my allowance saved for two weeks."

Lucinda knocked softly at the Browdowskis' door and waited what seemed a huge chunk of time. She stood on one leg, rubbing a stubby toe up and down it, wondering how she would tell them that Doctor Hitchcock was downstairs, black bag and all. When Trinket's father came to the door she began with the old formula: "How's Trinket this afternoon?"

Mr. Browdowski shook his head. For some reason he couldn't speak. He looked so thin, so troubled, so desperate, Lucinda blurted out what she had come to say. "I've got a doctor downstairs. He's our family doctor—best in the city. Don't say no. He's always made me well every time I was sick. Please let him take care of Trinket!"

And then strangely enough he said the same words Doctor Hitchcock had said a few minutes before: "I'm beaten."

Lucinda brought the doctor up. They went inside the small, bare room. While Doctor Hitchcock and Trinket's mother stood over the crib, talking, doing things, Lucinda and Mr. Browdowski stood with their backs against the door. Lucinda found herself putting her arms about his middle as she did Uncle Earle's, pressing her cheek hard into his stomach. His hands found their way to her hair, stroking it. She thought of that first time she had spoken to them; how yellow Trinket's curls had shown in the dark hallway and how Trinket's father had said he liked Lucinda's hair, black and sleek as a raven's breast. She looked up into his face and each smiled courage at the other.

The rest of the day—there wasn't much of it—remained blurred in Lucinda's memory. It began with a question of a bathroom and hot water. There was none on the third floor. So Trinket was brought down and put in Lucinda's bed. Doctor Hitchcock took off his coat and vest, his cravat, undid his collar and rolled up his shirt sleeves. "You look just as if you were getting ready for a fight," said Lucinda.

"That is what I'm getting ready for. The odds are all against me, Lucinda. You might as well know it now."

Once she watched Trinket's father go up to Doctor Hitchcock and say something in a low voice. The answer was the wrong one, she could tell that. The doctor shook his head and both men turned from each other with faces as set as pavement.

Back and forth to kettles of hot water in the work-room went the doctor, wringing out hot cloths that smelled funny. Trinket was wrapped in these and they came off and there were more hot cloths to put on. Lucinda thought it was a nasty performance and was sure she wouldn't have been as patient about it as Trinket was. The tiny girl lay very still without opening her eyes or making a whimper. But she breathed hard, and made as much noise at it as Doctor Hitchcock, hurrying back and forth. They let Lucinda give Trinket her medicine every half hour, first from one glass and then from another. She would put the teaspoon between Trinket's lips and say: "Drink this for the tall giraffe," and down it would go. She got where she could do it without spilling a drop.

Miss Nettie and Miss Peters came home. They took Doctor Hitchcock's place with the kettles and the cloths; and the doctor put on his things and said he would be back after dinner. Dinner came and went; Doctor Hitchcock came and stayed. Lucinda was put to bed on the small sofa, curled up under a blanket, not undressed. But she didn't go to sleep— not for a long time. She had almost had a tantrum when Miss Peters said: "You're to go downstairs and sleep in Miss Lucy's room. "I won't," said Lucinda; "I won't, I won't!" Doctor Hitchcock had settled it. "Let her stay. It's far better she should."

So she lay with eyes that blinked and saw as in a dream figures moving about, sitting down, getting up. She heard as from another world, whispers with no words hanging to them. Comfortables and pillows were brought and laid on the floor; sometimes Trinket's mother lay down, and sometimes Trinket's father; but Doctor Hitchcock spent the night on his feet.

It was the longest night. It had hundreds of hours and millions of minutes. When she couldn't keep quiet any

longer she uncurled from the sofa and came softly over to
the bed to see if Trinket looked any different. After a while
she fell asleep; only to waken with a terrific jerk that sent her
head bobbing from the pillow. Then she fell asleep, hitting
a great depth and a great silence. It took a good deal of shak-
ing to waken her. Doctor Hitchcock was bending over her.
He was saying something again and again. Understanding
came slowly. "The little girl is asking for you. She wants
something," he kept saying.

Lucinda's legs were asleep; they didn't want to hold her
up. Doctor Hitchcock put an arm about her and steered her
to the folding bed where she dropped on her knees and put
her chin on the coverlet, close to Trinket's face. "What do
you want Trinket? What can Cinda do?"

The tiny girl, pint-pot size, smiled a little. "Froggy," she
said.

Lucinda turned an eager face up to the doctor: "She wants me to sing. Shall I?"

The doctor plucked at his beard, hard; then he nodded and went over to a window, where the blackness of night was graying into the coming of day. The singing at the beginning was lumpy, and then Lucinda forgot Trinket was so very sick and sang lustily:

> "Froggy would a-wooing go,
>   Heigh-O, said Rowley;
> Froggy would a-wooing go
> Whether his mother would let him or no,
> With a rolly, polly, gammon and spinach—
>   Heigh-O, said Rowley."

Once Lucinda thought Trinket almost laughed; that was when she came to the Mousy's Hall. Soon after, Trinket's eyes closed and opened and then closed; and Lucinda whispered to Mrs. Browdowski: "She's going to sleep nicely, isn't she?" and went on with the last verse.

> "As Froggy was taking him over a brook,
>   Heigh-O, said Rowley,
> As Froggy was taking him over a brook,
> A lily-white duck came and gobbled him up
> With a rolly, polly, gammon and spinach;
>   Heigh-O, said Rowley."

Doctor Hitchcock lifted her up from her knees and turned her towards the sofa. "Get some sleep. You've helped a lot."

He tucked her under the blanket and drew his hand over her eyes, shutting them. She lay there tired, obedient, happy, in that state that is not sleep and is not waking. Something roused her, the absence of all movement, probably. She sat up. Nobody was in the room. She looked at the folding bed. It was empty.

Only for a moment was she puzzled. Then she understood Trinket had gone to sleep and they had carried her up to her own crib. Lucinda got up, stretched all over, toes to neck, like a waking kitten. She went to the window and stood there with her nose pressed flat against the glass. Looking down into the street she saw something she had never seen happen before: she saw the lamp-lighter pass and put out the lamp at the corner. That was interesting.

Hands on her shoulders made her turn. Doctor Hitchcock had come back into the room and she hadn't heard him. She was all excitement. "Come to the window, and see the lamps put out and the city wake up." And then, "Trinket's a lot better, isn't she? Do you know what I'd like to do? I'd like to go out into the city and see it really come awake."

"Get on your things." Slowly Doctor Hitchcock pulled himself into his vest and coat, buttoned his collar, tied on his cravat. He took out his doctor's book and wrote something in it, tore out the leaf and put it on the mantelpiece. "So they'll know where we are," he explained. Lucinda wanted to take her skates; she had never skated at daybreak in the city; but the doctor looked troubled. "How can my old legs keep up with roller skates? Have a heart, Lucinda."

Lucinda pulled a feather out of her pillow to blow at the first cross-street; that was what an Irish lad did, seeking his fortune. The feather blew eastward. "Can we go to the river —way over to the river?" she was amazingly eager, untired, by the night.

The doctor nodded, "But we'll rout out the cabman and the sleepy horses yonder." They belonged to a dilapidated hack drawn to the farther side of Broadway. The two got out at the East River; Lucinda had never seen it from the middle edge of the city. On the way they had passed wagons full of milk cans, wagons piled with morning papers. Loafers went skulking into the shadows of old buildings. The night patrol of the police was changing with the day patrol; and rattling by them went a black carry-all, sounding a gong. "What's that?" asked Lucinda.

"It's the Black Maria."

Lucinda giggled and said something that astonished the old doctor: "I almost had a ride in it one day."

The two skirted the river northwards to Jones Wood. On the black surface of the water ferryboats, with lights still shining, looking like illuminated beetles, scooted from their piers to Williamsburg and Long Island City. The doctor pointed out three islands: Blackwell's, Ward's and Randall's; and told Lucinda something of the sorry cargo they carried.

Beyond the river to the east the sky crimsoned, then paled into rose. Lucinda thought of the lovely words Uncle Earle had read from *Romeo and Juliet*—about night's candles burning out, and jocund day walking tiptoe on the misty mountain top. "It's walking tiptoe, for us, on the river," she said, slipping a hand into the doctor's pocket where he had thrust his.

A whirring of white and gray wings over the river, quite close, told them the gulls were rising from where they had been sleeping the night through on the surface of the water. Their shrill, plaintive cries filled the air. They swooped and mounted and swooped again, their wings bending seaward.

Inside his pocket the doctor's hand closed tightly over Lucinda's; his eyes were following the gulls' flight, so were Lucinda's. "Do you know what the Esquimos believe about death?" he asked quietly.

"No."

"They believe that when a person dies her soul becomes a

white gull. You see, it is given wings, to fly hither and yon, where it wills, free as a bird."

"It must be wonderful to fly—really fly," said Lucinda. "I've always wanted to."

The mass of gulls was fading into the rushing light of the day, but one laggard rose from the river, swung inland and passed no distance at all from where they were standing. Lucinda could see how white and smooth the feathers lay upon its breast, how strong its wings beat the air. She asked wonderingly: "And when it is tired of flying seaward will it mount clear to heaven?"

"I think it will."

Lucinda looked up into Doctor Hitchcock's face. Something spoke out of that silence that held them both so still they might have been part of the river-front instead of human beings. Suddenly Lucinda knew what the doctor had not wanted to put into words. It went through her and shook her as an earthquake shakes a city. What her eyes asked, the doctor's eyes answered; then he drew Lucinda into the compass of his arms and said: "We'll go home to my house and have some breakfast. Then I think Trinket's father and mother would be very glad if you stayed close to them for a while."

Lucinda took a long time before she spoke: "I could tell them about the gulls. That would be putting beauty into it, wouldn't it? Uncle Earle said there must be lots and lots of beauty to make it great, and it must be inevitable; that in the end it must all add up right. Do you think it will add up some day, Docor Hitchcock?"

"I think we must believe that. Otherwise, what would be the use of going on?"

Only once in the drive back to the doctor's door did Lucinda speak; then she said: "I hope I'll have my chance at being a gull. That would be better than roller skates."

Lucinda found Trinket's parents in the Misses Peters' parlor. Miss Nettie was giving them coffee. Lucinda sat down like a person grown suddenly ancient and wise and told about the morning. Her eyes were very dry and very bright; her voice lilted and rose, as if it had found wings. As she talked about the morning, she wanted it to sound as wonderful to them as it had been for her, especially the flight of that lone gull.

When she had finished Mr. Browdowski said a funny thing. "Thank you, my Lucinda. It isn't hard to see our Trinket with wings, cleaving the sky; but we haven't twenty-five cents to bury what she has left behind."

Afterwards, when they had gone to their own room, Lucinda made Miss Nettie explain. She had known nothing of funerals, burials, cemeteries. It was very hard to understand and rather awful to think you had to pay money out for such things. Suddenly she became very Aunt Emilyish, as she told Uncle Earle later. If money was needed, money there must be. Instead of skating to school she would skate over and see Uncle Earle.

She said nothing about it, but started off as usual. When she reached Aunt Emily's house Katie told her that her uncle had gone to his office. Where was that office? Kate got the address from mam'selle. It was a number on Broadway, right next to Ann Street. That was easy, thought Lucinda. She would skate back to Broadway and keep on skating till she reached the number.

And that is what she did—from Forty-Ninth to Ann Street she skated that late March morning. Block after block after block; there was no end to them. No longer were there wings to her skates; they hung like dead weights at the ends of her legs. She ran down the last ten blocks like a poorly made mechanical toy. She was dizzy and skated in jerky curves until a working man stopped her. "Look here, young one, what's the matter?"

"I've got to get to Uncle Earle's. I've got to." Lucinda said desperately. The man found out the number and putting an arm around her pushed her the rest of the way, got her inside the door of Uncle Earle's office. "Snoodie!" Uncle Earle was out of his swivel chair, emptying the room of two clerks, lifting her to his lap, and unbuckling the skates.

"I'll tell you in a minute," she said. "Now it's good just to rest and not think about it—not think about anything!" She leaned her head back and closed her eyes.

March 30th, 189–

I haven't written in my diary for a long time. Everything has been very mixed up. Uncle Earle did everything about the funeral. There were lots and lots of flowers, and I bought Trinket a little pair of white ankle-ties to wear, remembered that day in the toy shop. It was the ankle-ties on the dollies she loved best of anything.

I guess I've found out about a lot of things since I joined the orphanage—pawn-shops and Proctor's and other things, like death. Death is something grown up people try to keep children from knowing about. I think it's silly. So does Uncle Earle. What is hard to understand is how death divides you in two. Something goes and something stays. Perhaps I shall understand it better when I grow older, but Uncle Earle says nobody understands it very well.

April 10th.

I don't seem to want to write much. Everybody in the house is looking after Trinket's parents. And a very nice thing has happened. Mr. Night Owl did it. He took Trinket's father somewhere to play for some people, especially a man by the name of Thomas; and now he's going to play with an orchestra at real concerts. Miss Lucy, honey, has fixed up a nice room for them in her other house. The room upstairs is empty. Sometimes when I get home from school and it's rainy so I can't go out, I go up and sit on the top stair and play I am going to borrow Trinket again. Mama would think I was a

very silly little girl. I go to bed in my own bed, but after a
while I go and knock at the door and ask Miss Nettie if I can
get into bed with her. She always says: I was hoping you
would come, Lucinda and then we talk in whispers about
lots of things and I go to sleep in a jiffy. I do love Miss Nettie.

CHAPTER X

AWAY GOES LUCINDA

THAT spring was a resplendent one. Lucinda met it
with arms wide-flung when it came. She gathered it in
through every sense, made especially acute because a make-
believe princess and a little girl, pint-pot size, had gone
from her.

The happenings of every day stood like the writing on the
wall; they were important; they had a message for her. Trinket's parents needed her so often, and that fact above all else
filled her with a slow-mounting exultation. Her own parents
had never needed her that way; as a little girl she had never
been dreadfully important to them and she had known it

without fussing about it in the slightest. Her brothers—four, nine, twelve, and eighteen years older than she was—had absorbed the youth of her parents; as a household they were fixed and sufficient when Lucinda had made her impulsive appearance. She had not been counted upon, nor was she greatly wanted. She had been tempestuous from the first; and the family had grown inevitably into an attitude towards her. She knew while she was surprisingly young that they looked upon her as a difficult child; they thought her not pretty, given to tantrums, to be disciplined and endured. But beyond her family, in some vague place in the world, she had always hoped there would be people who would like her, who would want to have her 'round. Johanna, for example, was the one first to prove this hope for her.

And now Trinket's father and mother clung to her as if life could not go on for them without her. Mr. Browdowski took her with him when she could go to the rehearsals of the orchestra. No one paid any attention to her; but no one sent her home. She sat on a stool, sometimes moving it about where she could listen closer to what the horns were saying, to the violins, to the big bull fiddles, to the bassoons and the flutes. Going home afterwards she asked hundreds of questions and learned about symphonies and concertos and chorals; and the parts the different instruments played in them. Without knowing it she made the beginning of a musical education at a time when great music was supposed to be beyond the grasp of a young child.

The night that Trinket's father played at his first concert, Lucinda went with Trinket's mother. It made an impression Lucinda was never to forget. To watch so many bows drawn in unison across so many violins, to watch dozens of fingers running together over strings and stops, to wonder that one man, alone, should think up such music for so many to play. And the music itself! It emptied her completely of all her contents, as if she had been a box, a jug, a vase; and then it filled her full again of itself, to overflowing. It was at the end as if she were nothing but a container for it. Once only Lucinda whispered to Trinket's mother: "It's silly to believe that you learn everything at school. I know now what it meant in the Bible when it talked about the stars singing together. I've closed my eyes some of the time, and when I do that's what it is—the stars singing together. Johanna says the loveliest music in Ireland was caught by some lad going to sleep with his ear to a fairy rath. Do you suppose Beethoven went to sleep with his ear to the stars?"

While everybody took care of Trinket's parents, they took care of Lucinda as well. The elders of the two houses and some outside had a strong feeling that the losing of Doctor Hitchcock's fight that night had upset Lucinda's world for the time being. It had made her vulnerable to life as the holding of Achilles's heel when he had been dipped into the River Styx had made him vulnerable in that one spot.

So it happened that Vittore Coppino bought Tony a pair of roller skates, and he was free after school to go wherever fancy led Lucinda. They skated everywhere in the lower end of the Park, through the Merchant's Gate, out the Artist's Gate, in the Scholar's Gate, and around the pond. They fed the goldfish; they coasted down the Mall. They visited the monkey-house and made a special call upon Mr. Crowley, the pet chimpanzee. They rode the musical horses in the carrousel; a nickel a ride unless you caught the gold ring on the blade of your sword. Sometimes Lucinda did, and sometimes Tony. Once Tony got it three times running and Lucinda was so excited she trotted 'round and 'round, trying to keep even with him. For whoever got the gold ring got a free ride. Tony always rode a white horse, Lucinda a black one, and she called hers Pegasus.

They skated up to the Museum of Natural History and could never get their fill of it. "It's too big," said Tony one day in despair. "We will never, never see it all."

"It's a good thing it's big. There are enough things to see all in a minute. I like having something saved over for next time." Lucinda was in the North American Indian room; it had more fascination for her than any other. She pored over the exhibits and wished she had been born an aborigine. She couldn't enthuse Tony with her idea. "Be an Injun—wear feathers and go naked! Lucinda this is a craziness of yours. You can never be one."

"I know, but I'll always wish I could and ride a buffalo."

The first warmish Saturday Lucinda made sandwiches and

Tony dug the potato cans out of his cellar and they skated past Hunter's Gate to the empty lot. They had brought enough lunch to share with old Rags-an'-Bottles. Each added an extra potato in his can for him. They waited excitedly, craning their necks stiff, cocking their ears to catch the first jangle of bells. But old Rags-an'-Bottles, his cart and his horse, Minnie, never came. Neither child spoke out to the other his intense disappointment; each heart was troubled, wondering what had kept their adventurous companion away. The children never went back to the empty lot afterwards.

Aunt Ellen Douglas and Uncle Tom McCord took Lucinda with them on a Saturday night to see a musical comedy called *Robin Hood*. It took first place with *The Mikado* in Lucinda's theatrical treasure house. She saved all she could for two weeks from her allowance and took Tony. They saw it from the top balcony. She was captivated by it and wanted to keep going until she knew all the music by heart; it was such singing music. Some day she intended to use her old scenery and costumes and give *Robin Hood* all over again in the box theatre to the music of the Tinkers and Brown October Ale, of the Anvil Song and Oh, Promise Me.

She spilled her raptures upon Mr. Night Owl; and the very next night he came home with a libretto of the opera and gave it to her. Mr. Serge Browdowski, just beginning to be famous, helped her out by playing the airs on his violin, until she had the whole score by heart and could sing it from cover to cover.

The Solomons, like the Arabs, folded their costumes into their trunks and departed for the West. They were to play stock all summer. The two little girls parted with long promises of undying friendship and the future: "I'm going to be an actress some day. So will you, see if you don't. We'll meet on Broadway, sure as heaven." This from Aleda.

"I didn't know heaven was so sure," Lucinda smiled impishly. "But I guess I'd rather not be an actress. I wouldn't like saying the same thing over and over again. I'd rather write a play. I'll write it and you can act in it."

But there were moments when Lucinda was down-daunted, when she told Miss Nettie that she guessed if she couldn't borrow somebody-or-other she'd die. And then one afternoon she remembered the bambino—not the latest, but Gemma. She tore around to the Coppinos. She made Tony explain to his mother what she wanted and borrow from his father the push-cart he brought his fruit up in from the market. Triumphant, they stowed Gemma into the push-cart on a blanket and brought her over to the Misses Peters' parlor.

Miss Nettie was sewing at home that day and Lucinda burst into the work-room with Gemma hugged hard against her shoulder, her eyes shining: "It's the bambino, the one that was the bambino. Her nose has been dreadfully out of joint since the other one—Julius Caesar—arrived. And, Miss Nettie, I've got a perfectly elegant idea. She's got no clothes, none to speak of. Can't we make her some?"

Miss Nettie lifted Gemma from Lucinda's shoulder to her lap. She was an enchanting baby, her head covered with tight jet-black ringlets; her eyes as black and round as little pieces of polished jet; her face, round and chubby as a cherub's. She was born a coquette; her eyes flirted behind their heavy dark lashes, first with Lucinda, then with Miss Nettie.

The idea caught like wild-fire. Miss Nettie had lengths of cloth tucked into bureau drawers, and old dresses to be cut up. "It won't take a yard of goods hardly for a dress. Look at this," and she held up a white dimity, sprigged with rose-buds. That was the beginning of what Lucinda called the Bambino Sewing Circle. Mostly they sewed at night, and often Trinket's mother came and put stitches into what Miss Nettie insisted on calling a gertrude; though why Gemma should have a gertrude was beyond Lucinda.

Lady Ross supplied a somewhat worn flannel petticoat for underpinnings; and Miss Lucy, honey, contributed a length of pink ribbon for a bow to tie in Gemma's hair. The Sewing Circle made enough clothes to last Gemma out of babyhood. Eventually they were worn out by Cesare, whom Lucinda insisted always on calling Julius Caesar.

She borrowed Gemma often and loved to cuddle her, but the dolls' dishes were never brought out for her; and the *Saint Nicholas Song Book* stayed on the table, unopened.

On the last of April, the twenty-eighth to be exact, Uncle Earle took Lucinda to Daly's. It was the birthday of William Shakespeare—the special performance was *As You Like It*. All the best players were in it and there was a gala feeling to the crowd and the actors that got into Lucinda's blood and made her go all crinkly up and down her spine. She was very charitable towards Daly; as one producer should be towards another. Her tongue wagged constantly through all intermis-sions. "It's lovely. And of course, real actors can do things dolls can never do. But I do think, Uncle Earle, that our scenery was just as nice as theirs; and our costumes, I think, were a little better."

Uncle Earle agreed. Never had he seen Shakespeare better set up than it had been done on Twelfth Night past.

"Only," Lucinda equivocated, "the play is more real this way. I'm in that Forest of Arden this minute. I might be a brown rabbit, there among the trees, no one seeing me. I know all the big speeches and all the fun before it happens. It's that way with Aunt Emily. I always know ahead of time just what she's going to say, as if I'd learned her by heart."

Uncle Earle's laugh came with such an explosion that everybody around them turned to look, and Lucinda felt her cheeks grow very red and hot. She was glad to have the lights dim out and watch the curtain go up again. She never watched this happen that it did not leave her as breathless and spellbound as that time when she was six and had watched her first curtain go up on *The Mikado*.

One night, after supper, Lucinda stood up against the parlor door jamb and Miss Nettie marked her growing above the September height. Two inches she had grown and Miss Peters said her dresses were too short and her spring reefer wouldn't do, and she must have new things. So on a Saturday she and Miss Peters bought a coat and a new hat—a leghorn with pink apple-blossoms all around the brim. It was the prettiest hat Lucinda had ever had. She picked it out herself, hoping everybody would admire it as much as she did. And afterwards Miss Peters took her into Huyler's and they had chocolate sodas. Lucinda always got excited over a soda at Huyler's. To lean on the counter and gaze at the cake of ice with a red rose frozen inside always made her think of lovely things: like Snow White in her little crystal coffin; and Alpine climbers who had fallen down a crevasse and came out years afterwards in a Swiss glacier, looking fresh and perfect, just like the red rose.

The loveliest thing that happened that May was a wedding, with Lucinda as one of the four bridesmaids. Once before she had been bridesmaid, at her cousin Lucinda Wyman's wedding. Everybody had made great fun of it—that a little Lucinda should be standing up with a big one, and both named after their grandmother, a remarkable Lexington woman who had been born over a hundred years before Lucinda.

This second wedding belonged to Miss Claire Benton, the young and the pretty teacher at Miss Brackett's. She was to be married in the Church of the Messiah, and a rich aunt was giving her a wedding reception at Louis Sherry's. The bridesmaids were all children from Lucinda's class at school. They were to wear white fluffy organdie dresses with pink ribbon sashes; they were to carry gilded baskets full of pink roses.

"I don't see why you picked me out," Lucinda said bluntly at recess, catching Miss Claire in the hallway. "Aunt Emily says I'm homely as two toads, and the other girls are so pretty."

"Why Lucinda!"

"Well, look at me. Uncle Earle who loves me a lot says I'd have made a better papoose or bambino than I would an American child of high society. And Johanna always said my hair looked like a croppy-boy's. Beatrice Coudert has such lovely pink cheeks and golden curls, and so has Laura. And you know how perfectly elegant Virginia looks in her chestnut curls. I'll just about ruin the procession."

"You'll look perfectly elegant too, Lucinda." Miss Claire was looking at her with such a really fond look. "You're so alive and interesting—don't you think that's better than just being pretty?"

"Not for bridesmaids at a church wedding."

"But I want you, Lucinda; I want you the most of all."

So it was settled. The wedding came on a lovely late afternoon. The bride looked like an angel from heaven in a satin dress and a long tulle veil and a bouquet of lilies of the valley. The bridegroom didn't look like much to Lucinda; but that didn't matter, for nobody looked at him but the minister. Miss Claire gave the bridesmaids their pink sashes and their lovely baskets and little silver filagree pins that had come from Switzerland and that she put on her very own self in the vestry just before the procession began. She kissed them all and wished they might be as happy on their wedding day as she was on hers. And she whispered in Lucinda's ear: "I think you're going to grow up to be someone rather distinguished some day. I'm going to be proud to remember always that you were one of my bridesmaids."

It was very solemn and very beautiful, marching up in front of Miss Claire. The organ sounded so tremendous that Lucinda held her breath and got out of step two or three times. But she remembered about how they were to stand and poked Virginia into place. She was close enough to see the ring go on Miss Claire's finger, and she and Virginia helped Miss Claire, who was now Mrs. Somebody-or-other, put back her veil. Lucinda was surprised and perfectly delighted in the way the bridegroom kissed the bride—just as if he meant it.

The organ was very victorious after the wedding was over and it was easier to march out. Lucinda made a short prayer to herself that she would have a train as long, a veil as misty, and look half as lovely, so that her bridegroom would kiss her as if he meant it, too.

Afterwards at Louis Sherry's they ate chicken salad and Parker House rolls and all the ice cream and cake they wanted. Each took home a box of wedding cake with gold initials on it. Lucinda slept on hers and had a lovely dream.

She dreamed she turned into a white gull. She flew out of the window just as she had played at flying—as easy as anything. Straight for the East River she went and there close to Jones Wood, on the surface of the water, she found another white gull—a Trinket-gull—waiting for her. They skimmed the water; they skimmed the blue of the sky, down the river they went to the sea. Once the Lucinda-gull spoke to the Trinket-gull. "My mama and papa are on a ship on the ocean. Let's fly out to meet them. They'll be awfully glad to see us."

The next day came the letter from Lucinda's parents, saying they would be leaving Italy in a few days; they would be home almost as soon as the letter.

The Gedney House had a kind of ball on Decoration Day. Lucinda was invited. Miss Nettie made her a new dress to wear—a salmon pink china silk, accordion-pleated. She had always wanted an accordion-pleated dress but Lucinda's mother, like many another in those days, believed that choosing clothes for Lucinda was a divine right, her very own. Lucinda wore her crocheted lace collar that Johanna had brought her from Ireland; and Mr. Gilligan drove her down to the hotel and back. The hole in the top of the cab was kept open both ways.

On the return journey, comfortably sleepy but with excitement still running in her veins, she told Mr. Gilligan all that seemed important about the ball. "Just about everybody danced with me; there were quadrilles and lancers and the schottische and all. I'm glad Mr. Dodworth struggled with me. Did you ever go to dancing school, Mr. Gilligan?"

"I never did. But I was one of them young bucks who danced with every lass at the cross-roads. Name me a reel and I'll dance it for you."

"We'd better wait until we get home. Remember the first time you drove me up from the Gedney House?"

"Do I remember me own mother!" shouted Mr. Gilligan.

"You've been an elegant friend—you and Mrs. Gilligan. I hope we'll keep on being friends as long as we live."

"A wish wished on the full of the moon always comes true. Lean out carefully and look above your head."

Lucinda leaned out, and sure enough, hanging from the ribbon of the sky overhead was a ripe, full moon.

"Let's go over to Ireland together some day—you and me and Mrs. Gilligan and the hansom cab." Lucinda's eyes were dragging shut.

"Faith, the horse might be gettin' seasick. She's never took a sea voyage."

And that was the last Lucinda heard. Somehow Mr. Gilligan got her out of the cab and carried her the two flights up, laid her down carefully on the folding bed and said to Miss Nettie, sitting up: "'Tis yourself and myself ma'am that could be wishing ourselves back to ten years old, just. If we could put a spell on her asleep there and keep her as she is for

the rest of her mortal life! God bless her." He turned reluctantly out the door. "Good night, ma'am. In Ireland the spell
would work."

The last day of Lucinda's orphanage came. It came to her
as a terrific and a final thing; it was like the last day of Pom-
peii. In the afternoon she skated over to Eighth Avenue to
get Tony, and found him behind the stand. Vittore was ill;
Tony would have to mind stand all day, until late that night.

Sorrowfully Lucinda sat down on the box he offered her;
and laboriously they shelled out between them the few words
they had to say to each other.

"You'll come and see me, Tony?"

"Oh, I dunno."

"You'll meet me in the Park. We'll skate there."

"With that mam'selle person that's always hung on to
you?"

"Maybe she won't come back."

"Maybe she will."

Lucinda knew—the last maybe had it. "What if she does!"

"Think it'll be any fun skating with her tagging us?"

"I can come over and see you."

"Sure you can. If your mama lets you come. But don't you
come unless you come alone. We don't want stylish people
poking into our cellar."

All the time she had sat on the box Tony had stood scowl-
ing down at her. He wasn't the same Tony; well, she wasn't
the same Lucinda.

She got up at last. "I'm going."

She skated up Eighth Avenue and turned into the Park
through the Merchant's Gate. The red japonica was out, so

was the mock orange. The air was sweet with them. She skated by the ball-grounds. Nobody was playing yet. She skated by the Common and watched the sheep nibbling the fresh, spring grass, they kept it cropped, close as a lawn-mower.

What a fine thing it was that the city hadn't sold the Park that spring for a race track! It could be kept always and always now for babies and children. She had been so excited about it when Uncle Earle had told her, so fearful that it might be lost. Uncle Earle and Uncle Tom McCord had signed the petition to keep it a park always; and they had won. Why, she could skate there the rest of her life. The idea enchanted her.

She came to the carrousel and watched the children riding the musical horses. A flat-faced little girl with freckles was riding Tony's horse; a boy in Fauntleroy clothes was riding her Pegasus, his red sash whipping the air like a dynamite signal. Lucinda wanted to stick out her tongue at them. But she didn't. She skated on towards the reservoir and Cleopatra's Needle. She guessed Cleopatra must have hated sewing as much as she did if she'd had all her needles made that size.

Tomorrow her papa and mama would arrive. She was to drive over to Hoboken with Aunt Emily, crossing the ferry, best manners on. And after that she would be whisked off to Narragansett; that wouldn't be so bad. But when September came—then what? The answer to that was as easy as beginner's arithmetic.

Clump—chug—chirr—clump! Today the skates sang a sorry rhythm. She'd never belong to herself again—not until she married and got herself a husband, and then she'd belong to him. Suppose she kept on skating in the Park for ever and ever! Never went back to the Misses Peters' parlor, two flights up; never went to meet mama and papa with Aunt Emily tomorrow; never had another mam'selle. She could do it; she could do it, live like the lambs in the Park, be as free as air, never have tantrums, and she could cuddle all the babies in their prams. Her next birthday wasn't far off. Somebody else could have it—could be eleven who wanted to. She didn't.

She reached the reservoir and stopped, climbed the steps to the railing and looked into the still, placid water. Leaning over she could see her face reflected in it. She addressed herself solemnly: "Lucinda, how would you like to stay in the Park? How would you like to stay always ten? You could tell Tony and Uncle Earle, perhaps; and Mr. Gilligan. They'd keep the secret for you. Winter you would sleep with the bears in their caves and come out in the spring. Come out every single spring always ten years old, never any older. That's what I'd call a perfectly elegant idea!"